Every Imaginable
Shade of Gray

D1404593

Every Imaginable Shade of Gray

Ronda Schiff

To order additional copies of this book, contact:
Xlibris Corporation
1-888-795-4274
www.Xlibris.com
Orders@Xlibris.com
80649

For Jody and Emily

Acknowledgements

I am indebted to Isabel Byron for not letting me forget; to Deirdre Channing, Jean Emeson, Neddy McMills, Jill Mittelman, Jody Rudin and Emily Rudin for reading and re-reading without complaint; to Beryl Byman, Kimbeth Judge and Nancy Turpin, my writer's group accomplices; and to Alan Channing for the cover photo.

George

Margaret and John Strickland were on their front porch arguing when a New York City sanitation truck backed up and rolled over their three-year old son who was tooling around on his tricycle at the edge of the family's driveway. The loud grating noise of grinding bottles and cans masked the sounds of crushing metal, so for a few merciful moments, Margaret and John, and even the driver, weren't aware of the unfolding tragedy. That is, not until Helen Morgan, working in her garden directly across the street, looked up and screamed.

Clutching the railing along side the porch steps, Margaret swung around to see George's tricycle on its side, the handlebars flattened, amputated, lying in the grass a few feet away. A small rear wheel rolled down the street, stopped finally by a pile of leaves at the curb in front of the Davenport's house. Margaret stared open-mouthed, blinking at the blurred sight of John as he vaulted over the porch railing, knelt beside the truck and reached behind the wheel at the navy blue-and-white striped tee shirt she had pulled over the boy's head only an hour earlier.

Frozen, Margaret pressed her fists hard against her mouth while the driver, gesturing frantically, shouted at Helen Morgan to get help.

Within minutes, two police radio cars, a fire engine and an ambulance raced up the block. Sergeant Ed Burns coaxed the Stricklands into the back seat of his car before following the ambulance to the hospital. For months afterward, Margaret re-lived that frenzied ride—the desperate pleading with God, the whispered Hail Marys, the uncontrollable trembling of her hands, the nausea . . . and finally, the paralyzing fear at the sight of the small lifeless body.

When these memories eventually faded, she grappled with those that refused to fade—the shrill hysteria in Helen Morgan's scream and the argument with John that had forced her attention from George. She remembered these two things with astonishing clarity.

In the days that followed, friends and neighbors filled the Strickland's small house on Wentworth Street. The Flynns from next door, the Ansfields whose son Steven played with George, John's high school friend Peter Desmond and his wife Carla . . . and Helen Morgan, whose lacerating scream would reverberate in Margaret's nightmares for years to come. They brought food, casseroles, trays of sliced deli meats, cookies, fruit.

John's younger sister Elyse arrived with their mother. A heavy-set woman in her fifties, Estelle Strickland had been George's only grandparent. Her husband, disabled by a series of strokes, had died the previous year. Despite her grief, Estelle brought order into the house, quietly clearing tables, wrapping food and washing dishes.

John marveled at his mother's steady bearing, at her resigned acceptance of things fundamentally unacceptable, at her unflappable stoicism. Five years after his own birth, Estelle had lost an eleven-month old child to pneumonia, his baby sister Nicole. He could still picture Estelle genuflecting in the pew at the church funeral service, her unwavering eyes fixed on the priest. Over the years, she had buried two of her brothers and, last year, her husband. Now her only grandchild. John felt reassured by the sight of her at the kitchen sink, with Margaret's flowered apron spanning a mere fraction of her wide girth. He latched onto a vague and dwindling hope that he and Margaret would find strength and resilience similar to hers.

Margaret's brother Will flew in from Chicago where he lived and worked for Prudential Insurance. When Prudential had offered him the position a few weeks after his college graduation, Margaret and John had taken him out to celebrate, wrecking their month's budget for a fancy lobster dinner in Sheepshead Bay. John had taken two vacation days to help Will make the drive from New York to Chicago. The two of them drove off in the U Haul as Margaret waved from the curb and wept.

Will was her only living relative. Together they had navigated a childhood nearly ruined by their father's incessant and roiling anger, erupting with stunning frequency through the years. If the beef stew wasn't hot enough or his cigarettes not within immediate reach . . . no reason was too flimsy.

In the days after the funeral, Margaret and John barely spoke. At night in bed, John moved closer to her, aching to feel some comfort. Unresponsive, she lay with her back to him, too depleted to feel the anger that would later hover around her like thick, toxic air. She blamed the accident on John. Hadn't she been walking down the front porch steps toward George when John stopped her? Yes, she remembered doing exactly that. But then, his insistent voice demanding to know about the car, needlessly reminding her that she'd wrecked the same fender only a few months earlier in Waldbaum's parking lot.

It wasn't her fault this time, she said, exasperated at having to explain herself again. She was half-way through the sentence when Helen Morgan screamed.

Each night, they lay next to each other in strained, suffocating silence. With her eyes closed, Margaret pictured George's round, almost chubby face, his bright blue eyes, the freckles scattered across his nose. She imagined herself combing his hair, light brown and stick straight, wetting the back to tame the stubborn cowlick. When she cried, John inched closer and held her. When she woke in the middle of the night shivering, he held her again. He had no idea of what to say. He chafed against the unthinkable notion that she held him responsible, but in her aloofness, in her lack of eye contact, he felt the unspoken blame.

Each morning John got up early to make coffee. He'd wait at the kitchen table for Margaret, listening for the slapping sound of her slippers on the stairs, hoping that this would be the morning, finally, she'd smile and kiss him loudly on the back of his neck, part of their morning ritual.

It didn't happen.

After a full week had passed, John forced himself up the stairs, passing the closed door of George's room on his way to theirs. He sat on the bed next to Margaret, gently touching her arm. "Maggie." The nickname only he was allowed to use. "Come down. The coffee's ready."

"Not now," she said, pressing the back of her hand against her forehead.

This was new to him, these shards of icy, clipped words. He took a deep breath. "It has to be now. Tomorrow I'm going back to work." This declaration, completely unplanned, startled both of them.

She smelled after-shave and saw from his wet hair that he had already showered. "Tomorrow?" Her voice hoarse and breathless. Her eyes lingered on the bump at the bridge of his nose, broken years ago in a high school basketball game.

He nodded. "I'm not doing anything here. I need to be doing something."

She looked away. She had left her own job as a fifth grade teacher at four months pregnant with George. She remembered John there, leaning unexpectedly against the fence at the school playground, his curly brown hair blown to one side by the wind. John, smiling, always the thoughtful one. He had left his job early to cheer her up on her last day of work. On their way to the subway, he had coaxed her into Shackley's for a root beer float, her favorite.

"You don't even look at me," his voice broke through her memory. "Sometimes I think you blame me." His almost-pleading eyes riveted on her face.

Margaret clutched the blanket, pulling it up to cover her shoulders. She knew better than most the power of words lashed out in careless anger. She had struggled, uselessly, to overcome her father's stinging sarcasm, the demeaning, caustic comments he had flung at her, at her mother and brothers.

"I don't blame you," she said lamely, forcing herself to look at him. "I just . . . I don't know . . . I can't . . . ." She bit her lower lip.

Reaching for her hands, John looked at her, her eyes red and swollen, the skin taut around her mouth. He felt her slipping away from him.

"Maggie, please. I'll make breakfast. We can go for a walk."

In the kitchen, Margaret settled her eyes on the table, on yesterday's toast crumbs, on the butter dish. John watched her expectantly though she made no effort to talk. She wanted to see George next to her in his booster seat, his cereal half-eaten. She remembered at lunch, a mere few weeks ago, he had turned to her and said, "Mommy, how many sleeps 'til Grammy comes?"

Margaret had pressed his cheeks between her hands. "You are so cute," she had said, beaming at him.

"Mommy, you're cute," he'd said, laughing.

The booster seat, now gone, taken by Will to the attic before he'd gone back to Chicago. She glanced at John and remembered again how she had stopped at those porch steps and turned her back to George.

As they walked out of the house, John took her hand. It was limp and tentative, a reluctant participant. He held onto it tightly as if he could will it to respond. They walked slowly down Wentworth Street, a quiet block in a middle-income section of Queens, lined on both sides by identical brown brick houses, each with a front porch like their own. Everywhere there were reminders—a pair of roller skates carelessly dropped on a front lawn, a woman pushing a baby carriage, a little girl shoveling dirt into a small red wagon. Before they had gone two blocks, Margaret was crying. John himself felt like crying. How would they ever go on? They turned back.

At home, Margaret ran up the stairs to the bedroom. John sat in the wooden rocking chair on the front porch, staring from a distance at the spot where George had been hit. He stayed there until a sanitation truck rounded the corner and began to make its way toward his house. Then he got up and went inside.

At dinner, Margaret sat at the table, not eating, not speaking. "You've hardly eaten anything for days." John's voice was gentle.

Her eyes flashed at him. "Do you think I care what happens to me?" Sudden anger sliced through her voice.

John took a deep breath. "I care what happens to you," he said softly. He felt himself sinking and dropped his gaze to the table.

The next morning he went to work. When Margaret heard the garage door close, she got out of bed. On her way downstairs, she stopped at George's bedroom door. She pictured him asleep in his bed, clutching his blue blanket, his two teddy bears on either side of his pillow. She thought back to the Easter Sunday, more than a year ago, when they'd left one of the bears at Estelle's house. George had cried inconsolably, walking from room to room, his thumb in his mouth, dragging his blue blanket on the floor behind him. Before long, John was back in the car, making the 20-minute drive to retrieve the teddy bear. Margaret pressed her fists against her temples. For a dented fender she had turned away.

She returned to her room, made the bed and drew open the curtains. Seeing the swing set in the yard, she quickly shut her eyes. Only last year, Will had come to the house with it, twenty-eight pieces in all, a gift for George's second birthday. He had spent most of the afternoon assembling it.

Restless, Margaret went back downstairs. Retrieving a rag from the broom closet, she carefully dusted the living room furniture, the two mahogany end tables that she and John had bought at a garage sale just after they were married. They had carried them home, one at a time, John walking backwards, laughing. It had been the sound of his laugh—unrestrained, full of energy—that had lassoed her attention in a Brooklyn College lecture hall nearly six years earlier. Their class in Russian History had just ended. John, laughing with his friends a few rows in front of her, had turned around in time to see her smiling at him.

She knelt down to reach the wooden claw-like feet on the sofa, then the coffee table with a jagged scratch from George's dump truck. He and Steven Ansfield had been playing with their trucks next to this same table just a few months ago. Margaret had been in the kitchen spreading peanut butter and jelly on a plate of Ritz crackers when George peeked in from behind the door.

"Mommy," his blue eyes wide, his lower lip puckering. "My bad bad truck did a bad thing."

Dropping the rag, Margaret went back into the kitchen and filled a pail with hot water and a splash of ammonia. Down on her hands and knees, she washed each individual yellow linoleum square. When she was done, she made a piece of toast, another cup of tea and looked up at the clock. It was barely 10 am. How would she get through the day?

*   *   *

It was John's sister Elyse who, after more than a year, coaxed them into joining a group for grieving parents. She went with them on that first Tuesday evening to a community center a few blocks from their house where the weekly meetings were held.

Every week after, Margaret and John went and listened to the other couples. After several sessions, Geraldine and Bob Pascarelli spoke, voices faltering even after seven years, about arriving home from a party one Saturday night to find their smoldering house surrounded by firefighters, their three children in the hospital. By the time they got to the emergency room, the two youngest had already died. The oldest, a daughter, had spent three months in the Cornell Medical Center burn unit and subsequently underwent multiple skin-graft surgeries. The following week, the Pascarelli's brought their daughter Corrine, now 24. Margaret stifled a gasp when she saw Corrine's face, rippled with scarring. Reflexively, she reached for John's hand. He pulled her close and she buried her face in his chest. Seeing Corrine face softened something in Margaret. Geraldine and Bob Pascarelli had begun to recover. Why couldn't she?

Week after week, Margaret and John went to the meetings. Wordlessly he watched her, his eyes tracking her movements, her facial expressions, as she sat hugging herself, her arms crossed in front of her. She watched the other couples as they stood to tell their stories, wincing at the pain in their faces and in their quavering voices. She shuddered at the sight of their trembling hands clutching cherished, worn snapshots. She admired, even envied the others as they spoke of struggling forward. They got themselves out of bed in the mornings, returned to their jobs, took care of their other children.

After the meetings, John held onto her arm as they walked home. Her silence chilled him, filling his chest with a dull ache. He wanted to break through it, to find a way back to the easy effortless flow of unforced conversation. "Do you think we should talk . . . at the next meeting?" he asked cautiously.

"No!"

His suggestions, almost all of them, fizzled in the face of her automatic negative responses. He swallowed hard and moved closer, slipping his arm around her waist. Her body relaxed. At least that, he thought. At least that.

*   *   *

Seventeen months after George's death, John and Margaret made love. Two-and-a-half years later, Vanessa Strickland was born. In the first month, John brought home gifts several times a week. He filled her room with dolls and stuffed animals. Over her crib, he hung a mobile made of brightly-colored quilted cotton shapes, giraffes, elephants, butterflies, fish. For her dresser, he found a music box that played **Twinkle, Twinkle, Little Star**. He bought floating bath toys, an array of rattles, teething rings, cloth-covered alphabet and number books, fairy tales.

Margaret, desperate to feel the joy she had known at George's birth, felt only a dense enervating despair. She began to nurture a growing resentment toward John, so completely consumed by the presence of this new baby. Had he forgotten? He was the one who had started the argument, demanding at that singular moment to hear about a meaningless dent in a car they traded-in a year later. If not for that, she would've been in the driveway with George. She would've seen the garbage truck backing toward him. She could have pulled him out of the way.

Weeks passed. She watched them both, John and Vanessa, with envy. She berated herself for having the baby who, for John, had supplanted

George. She clenched her teeth when John came home from work carrying another gift-wrapped package. The veins in her forehead throbbed, her neck and jaws ached. She knew he didn't wake abruptly in the night to the sound of Helen Morgan's scream. It wasn't fair.

Almost four years later, Grace was born. Margaret's brother Will flew in from Chicago and, with John's mother Estelle, stayed at the house to take care of Vanessa. Will was holding Vanessa's hand when she leaned over to look at the new baby in her mother's arms. The four adults watched, dumbfounded, as Vanessa's arm jutted out, her little fingernails scratching two thin lines across Grace's cheek. Grace cried out, the frail, unsteady cry of a newborn. Margaret screamed at John, her face twisted with disgust, "Get her away from here!"

John pulled Vanessa to his side. "My god, Maggie! She's just a child." He looked at his wife, his eyes wide, disapproving.

"You let her do whatever she wants," she said quietly, embarrassed by her outburst. Cautiously she looked back at him, then at Will and Estelle, and finally at Vanessa.

"I'm sorry. I'm just very tired." She held out her hand to Vanessa. "Vanessa, come help Mommy put baby Grace in the crib."

"No!' shouted Vanessa, wide-eyed, clinging to her father's leg.

*   *   *

Before leaving for Chicago, Will cornered Margaret in the kitchen. "I'm not sure how to say this," he whispered, "but you've got to get a hold of yourself."

She looked at the window over the sink and out to the back yard, gritting her teeth at the sight of the swing set. She was exhausted, her stitches hurt. She pressed the back of her hand against her forehead.

"Remember when you came here and set up the swing for George?" she asked. Her eyes searched his face, a face that still reminded her of the scared little boy she had taken to school on his first day of kindergarten, clutching his small hand in her own. She wanted to see the dimpled smile she had always envied, to hang onto what she sensed was his fading admiration.

He put his hands on her shoulders, gripping them tightly. "Margaret," his voice insistent. "I'm talking about Vanessa. You don't like her. I've only been here two days and I can see it. What's worse . . . she sees it. And the tension between you and John . . . I'm afraid for you, Margaret. I really am."

She forced her eyes to meet his, her lips tightly pursed, pinched together in a thin line.

"You can turn this around. I know you can," he said, his voice softer now.

Margaret covered her face with her hands. What could she say to him? That Vanessa had none of George's sweetness. That she was stubborn and petulant. That she often turned away from Margaret and ran to John. Finally, she looked at Will. "I don't know . . . when George died, I felt so angry . . . all the time. And John . . ."

Will cut her off. "John is a good man, Margaret. You are lucky to have him. Whatever else you feel, just put it aside."

*   *   *

Margaret began watching John and Vanessa together, listening to his easy encouraging tone as he ran down the street next to her, his hand holding the bicycle steady so she wouldn't fall. From the porch, Margaret could see them laughing when they reached the corner. Vanessa, letting the bike fall, threw her arms around her father's waist. John's face relaxed

into the broad smile that, for years, had made Margaret feel cherished. She
closed her eyes. Will had been right. She promised herself, she would try
harder.

But, somehow, her best intentions unraveled when she was alone with
Vanessa and Grace. No sooner did she get them dressed to go to the park,
Vanessa would sit down on the floor and untie her shoe laces. She'd grab
Grace's bottle of apple juice and drink from the freshly washed nipple.
Margaret would re-tie Vanessa's shoes, rinse the nipple and turn around to
find Vanessa on the floor untying her shoes again.

On days they were stuck at home, Vanessa began playing with the
toilet paper, walking long trails of it through the house, wrapping it around
the furniture. Exasperated, Margaret locked the downstairs bathroom. In
response, five-year old Vanessa left a puddle of urine on the floor outside
the locked door.

At the playground, Vanessa blossomed into the neighborhood trouble
maker. She grabbed toys from the younger children, filled her pail with sand
and dumped it, sometimes flung it, out of the sandbox. If the swing she
wanted was taken, she jumped up and down crying. One day, she pushed
the Delaney's baby carriage into the sprinkler, with three month-old Billy
Delaney asleep in the carriage.

The other mothers complained to Margaret. They expected her to
control Vanessa. They didn't go to the park to stand guard over their
children.

Margaret tried. She offered Vanessa rewards for behaving well—an ice
cream cone, a small toy. After awhile, these little bribes stopped working.
Margaret, forced to watch Vanessa closely, jumped up whenever she might
need to intervene. When Vanessa shoved one of the other children, Margaret
grabbed her arm and pulled her away. Vanessa, trying to twist free, sunk
her teeth into her mother's hand.

Struggling to stifle her own mounting anger, Margaret stared at Vanessa, feeling hot with shame before an audience of toddlers and their disapproving mothers. In front of everyone, she had been rebuffed by her own five year-old child . . . who was supposed to need her.

She stopped taking Vanessa and Grace to the playground although she disliked staying home, barely mustering the energy to keep the girls occupied in the back yard or the basement family room. She took them to the library on Wednesday mornings for children's story hour and once a week on a bus to Estelle's house. Estelle cheerfully made ginger snap cookies and, Vanessa's favorite, macaroni and cheese. She'd spread old newspapers on the kitchen table and let Vanessa make a mess with the finger paints. When the paint dripped on the floor, Vanessa would jump off her chair and trudge through it. Estelle then smiled with pride at the small footprints in bright primary colors on her freshly washed floor.

"Grammy, come look," Vanessa would say, beaming at her grandmother and waving her paint-smeared hands in the air.

Estelle would smile back at her, watching her paint as she held Grace in her lap. "Gracie, do you see what your big sister's doing? She's making a beautiful picture."

With her pacifier bobbing energetically in her mouth, Grace reached toward the paints, while Margaret, feeling overmatched by her mother-in-law in a hundred different ways, sunk deeper into herself. All she could do was look on in silent envy and shudder at thoughts of her own inadequacy.

Grace

Even now, some thirty-five years later, I remember the anger looming, threatening, as my parents' raised voices reverberated through the house. I could hear them well beyond their closed bedroom door, the continuous rehashing of the same argument over my sister Vanessa.

"You let her do whatever she wants . . . you never discipline her . . . no wonder she always runs to you!" My mother's shrill voice, too often amplified by frustration.

"She runs to me because you pick on her—all she hears from you is criticism!" My father, somewhat more controlled, yet insistent with emphatic denials.

Resentment over Vanessa was my parents' foremost irreconcilable difference. I should know—I'm her younger sister, Grace.

The growing rift between them caused inescapable tension for all of us. When we went out together, my father automatically took Vanessa's hand and my mother, needing an ally, took mine. I used to imagine some giant gloved fingers gripping an over-sized pair of scissors and cutting decisively through the center of our family picture, the one taken last Christmas. Two of us on each side, a clean split.

With a knot in my stomach, I would watch my father and Vanessa laughing together. There was no laughter from my mother, just her unpredictable moods and icy silences—and her unforgettable clenched teeth.

One hot summer Sunday at the zoo, Vanessa and I watched with delight as the monkeys chased each other around their cages. Our parents, sitting together on a park bench a distance away, were, oddly enough, smiling at each other. As we approached and they shifted to look at us, my mother's smile turned first to a frown then to a grimace when she saw Vanessa. My father's face, his eyes also on Vanessa, radiated pride. I stopped walking and there, at the Bronx Zoo, my five year-old mind began to process my relative insignificance to both of them.

"Go buy yourselves some ice cream." My father, squinting into the sun light, held a dollar bill in his outstretched hand.

Vanessa threw her arms around his neck, brushing her face against his curly brown hair. "Come with us, Daddy," She said, taking his hand and tugging at him to get up. She watched my mother, whose lips suddenly looked glued together in a tight thin line, her eyes narrowed on Vanessa. The three of us walked toward the refreshment stand, Vanessa in the middle holding hands with both of us, turning around twice to look at my mother.

When we went back, the bench was empty. My father looked around, his face strained, glancing first at his watch, then scanning the benches lining the walkway. I watched him nervously as we ate our ice cream, my stomach churning with worry over the possibilities awaiting us at home. Inches away from me on the bench, Vanessa smiled broadly, licking her ice cream and swinging her legs, her blond pony tail bouncing from shoulder to shoulder.

"Maybe we should go home now," my father said as soon as we finished.

"No!" Vanessa nearly shouted it. "We haven't seen the lions or the bears."

Two hours later, we walked into the still house. My mother was in her bedroom, the door locked. The next morning, the neatly folded sheets and pillow were stacked on the couch where my father had slept. Vanessa and I went to school without seeing her. When we returned, the bedroom door was still closed.

I don't recall how long she stayed up there, but when she finally spoke, it was to let me know how I had let her down. I remember her exact words with unmistakable certainty. I had chosen Vanessa and my father over her. I had dared to go for ice cream while she was left alone—discarded was the word she used—on the park bench. She expected nothing from Vanessa and not much from my father, but I was supposed to be on her side.

Her anger terrified me and not just in those early years. It was enormous and intractable, not softened by apologies or the tears of a young child. It seemed fused in her bones and hardened her face. Even years later, when time and age had diminished her rage, it was this earlier face that held fast in my memory.

I had trouble getting to sleep that night. Sometime after midnight, I finally went to Vanessa's room, piled her various stuffed animals at the foot of the bed and climbed in next to her. She didn't wake up, but feeling the warmth from her body comforted me.

The next morning, I remembered this dream:

My mother sent me to the store to buy a ten-pound sack of potatoes. Struggling under the weight, I made my way home slowly, stopping often to soothe the ache in my arms. Finally I rounded the corner to my block. My house was not there. All of the houses on the block were there but mine. I dropped the potatoes and rang a neighbor's bell.

*   *   *

In the second grade, I joined the Brownie troop at school. At the first meeting, Mrs. Lee, the troop leader, told us to line up and print our names on the attendance sheet. When my turn came, I wrote GRACE STRICKLAND in careful block letters. Seeing my name, Mrs. Lee rolled her eyes. "Are you Vanessa's sister?" she asked.

I came to understand that being Vanessa's sister was something I had to overcome, an inherited liability. Already, by age seven, I felt tainted by her reputation. I sometimes overheard other kids talking about her. She was angry at Judy Drucker's older sister and had ripped some pages out of her notebook. She elbowed Arlene Harris out of the way to be in the front row of the music class photograph. She spilled soda on MaryAnn Vesey's water color drawing, selected over Vanessa's own art work for a class contest.

Despite it all, I felt a strong loyalty to Vanessa. If something upsetting happened at school, it was her I sought out for comfort. "Don't worry, Gracie. It'll be okay." I can still hear her saying it.

In her own way, she watched out for me, walking me home from school, teaching me to roller skate, quizzing me for my Friday spelling tests. And yet, there was that other side to Vanessa, that disconcerting ability she had to turn in an instant, to lash out without warning. With Vanessa, I never knew what was coming next.

*   *   *

When she was in sixth grade, Vanessa entered a contest at school to create an art project for the Thanksgiving display at the main school entrance. She drew a painstaking picture of the Mayflower, modeled after a rendering in her history textbook. She spent hours at the desk in her bedroom, drawing, erasing, re-drawing. Sometimes I went in there and watched her working on it as she chewed on strands of her blond hair pulled loose from her pony tail. When she was finally satisfied, she colored it with felt tip pens. Proudly, she put her initials at the bottom right corner—VMS—Vanessa Meredith Strickland.

The first-place prize went to Suzanne Springer who lived five houses down from us on Wentworth Street. She had made a life-sized turkey from pieces of colored felt and glued them to a large poster board cut into the shape of a turkey. The entire thing was attached to wooden legs and appeared to be standing when propped up against the wall.

The winner's name was announced during a school assembly. All the kids clapped when Suzanne went up onto the stage to get her prize. I looked around the auditorium for Vanessa and finally saw her staring straight ahead, her teeth clenched and her upper lip curled into a sneer.

When we walked home from school together later that day, Vanessa was unusually quiet. Finally, I said, "I'm sorry you didn't win. Your picture was really good."

"No big deal," she said dismissively. "I didn't really care about it anyway."

A few days later, Vanessa and I saw Suzanne walking behind us, carrying home pieces of her felt turkey, cut into jagged ribbons with a pinking shears. Out of the corner of my eye, I saw a flicker of the smirk on Vanessa's face before she covered it with her hand.

*   *   *

For my ninth birthday, Grandma and Aunt Elyse took us to dinner at Lim's, a neighborhood Chinese restaurant. The six of us sat in a large round booth and ordered my favorite dishes. After dessert, Mr. Lim, the owner, brought over three large balloons tied to colored strands of ribbon. As if on cue, colorfully-wrapped presents materialized in front of me. I picked the one from Grammy off the top of the pile, a small box covered with silver paper and white ribbon. Inside, carefully laid on a mound of silver satin was a beautiful gold locket on a delicate chain. I wore it faithfully until the day I lost it, almost seven years later. Changing for gym, I discovered the broken chain caught in my waist band, the locket gone. All the girls in my class crawled around the gym floor on their hands and knees looking for it. Weeks passed before I dredged up the courage to tell my grandmother.

My mother gave me a bright red cardigan sweater with pearl white buttons. From Aunt Elyse, I got a baking set with pre-mixed chocolate cupcake batter, vanilla frosting and a cupcake tin. Vanessa gave me a set of water color paints. Even the people at the next table, having shifted in their seats to watch me open the presents, wished me a happy birthday.

Later that evening, my father led us down to the family room in the basement. My mother, Vanessa and I stood, our eyes closed, in front of a large bulging structure with an old sheet draped over it. At my father's signal, we opened our eyes to see a magnificent doll house, nearly four feet tall. Each room was fully furnished, right down to match-sized logs in the fireplace. The dining table had been set with miniature dishes and silverware. Pots and pans were stacked on the stove against the wall. It must've taken him days to assemble.

I didn't realize it was for me until my father smiled at me and said, "Happy birthday, Grace."

"Daddy!" I ran to him, throwing my arms around his waist. "It's beautiful! Thank you!"

I turned around to see Vanessa and my mother both glaring at him. I knew Vanessa wanted the dollhouse for herself; she wanted everything for herself. My mother was angry, I later overheard her tell him, because the sweater she gave me seemed inconsequential by comparison.

My mother did not speak to my father for three days. I still wince at the memory of her anger, how she ground her teeth until her jaw trembled, refusing to make eye contact, freezing all of us out. Her anger cast an indiscriminate net, ensnaring the guilty and innocent with equal venom. At these times, I would tiptoe nervously through the house, peeking into each room, doing everything I could to stay out of her way.

The next day after school I took Bert and Ernie, my two life-sized Sesame Street characters, and sat with them in the chairs at the doll house dining table. I filled the teapot with water and poured make-believe tea in each of our cups. I could hear Vanessa upstairs sulking, slapping magazines on tables, slamming doors. Then, directly above me, I heard my mother's footsteps on the kitchen floor and held my breath, expecting her to yell at Vanessa. Instead the back door slammed. I inched myself to the top of the stairs in time to see my mother backing the car out of the driveway. When she was gone, I ran up the stairs to Vanessa's room and knocked on her closed door.

"What?" she snapped. Her eyes were red, her face flushed.

"Vanessa, please come down. We can have a tea party."

"I'm not interested in that stupid doll house. It's for babies. Ask one of your baby friends." She pushed the door closed. I went to my own room and lay down on the bed.

The next day, I invited a classmate, Erin Stevens, to come home with me after school. We took the pillows off the couch in the family room and built a fortress around the doll house. It was Erin's idea to use Bert and Ernie as guards outside the fortress. Then we ran up to the kitchen for a bag of potato chips and some soda. Laughing and talking, we sat at the doll house dining table and cut out pictures from a stack of old magazines. At 4:30, we went upstairs to wait for Erin's mother.

The following day, I was back in the doll house alone looking through the pictures we had cut out and taped one, a litter of kittens, to the wall in the doll house living room. I looked around, trying to think of something else to do. It wasn't fun, playing there by myself. Quietly I climbed the stairs. I heard music on Vanessa's radio, playing behind her closed door. I went to my own room and started my homework.

About ten days later, I returned from school to find one side of the dollhouse completely collapsed. Inside, the dining table had been overturned; the miniature dishes lay broken on the floor. Even the little match-stick logs had been scattered over the area rug in the doll house living room. I sat down on the floor and cried.

Later Vanessa, who had refused to go down to the basement all week, appeared in the doorway. Looking at the wrecked house, she gasped in a way that I knew, even then, was not believable. Then she walked over and put her arm around me. "Oh, Grace. She probably did this while we were in school. You must hate her."

I slipped out from under her arm and ran up the stairs to my bedroom.

*   *   *

By the time Vanessa entered junior high school, our sporadic weekend family excursions had dwindled to occasional drives to see my grandmother. Otherwise, my father went to his office to catch up on his paper work or he played tennis with his friend, Mr. Desmond. Vanessa joined the drama club at school and usually went there on Saturdays to help build sets and make costumes. Sometimes I went with her to the park where she met a few other girls to practice baton twirling. Try-outs for the majorettes were to be held in the spring, and Vanessa was near desperation in her desire to make the team. My mother spent her weekends volunteering at the community center where she and my father had joined a support group after George died.

Vanessa and I knew about George, of course, although little more than the fact that he died at the age of three. I sometimes walked into the living room to look at the picture of him, still on the third glass shelf of the wall unit next to pictures of us. It was hard for me to imagine having this brother—a stranger—older than I, yet just a little boy.

Years earlier, Vanessa and I had discovered a cardboard carton in the attic with some of George's things—a red fire truck, a set of blocks with letters of the alphabet in black, two teddy bears and a blue blanket. We brought the blocks down to Vanessa's room and stacked them on the floor. When my father saw them, he knelt down next to us and whispered: "We better put these back upstairs. It will upset your mother to see them."

So Vanessa and I knew not to ask my mother about George. But over time, as she started increasing her hours at the center, she began mentioning his name. Just little comments—"George could count to twenty by the time he was two." Or "George had the most beautiful smile." I started looking in the mirror over my dresser, examining my smile from every angle, wondering what I could do to make it beautiful.

Years later, my tenth grade English teacher gave us vocabulary words to define and use in sentences. One of the words was melancholy. I wrote in my notebook: "MELANCHOLY: a tendency to be sad, depressed, gloomy. My mother is filled with melancholy."

Mrs. Ritter, my teacher, said: "Grace, your sentence does not demonstrate the meaning of melancholy."

You wouldn't say that if you knew my mother, I thought to myself.

*   *   *

Gradually my focus shifted from my family to my friends. Andrea Jaeger, Erin Stevens, Molly McGann and I would take the bus to the Esquire movie theater on Northern Boulevard. In the winter, we spent most of our Saturday afternoons there, eating buckets of buttered popcorn and, if the movie was boring, running up and down the aisles to find other friends from school. When the weather was nice, we rode our bikes to the park or went roller-skating.

By this time, Erin Stevens and I had become best friends. Every May since the first grade, she had come to my birthday parties carrying a neatly wrapped package tied with ringlet-curled ribbon. Back in the second grade, she had slept at my house one Friday night, and we made popcorn with Vanessa and watched a movie on TV. Then the three of us pulled the mattresses from the twin beds and crammed them onto the limited floor space in my bedroom, telling ghost stories and giggling well into the night. It was one of my happier childhood memories.

All week, I anticipated Saturday afternoons with my friends and was always disappointed when something interfered. When December arrived, the three of them were busy with their families every weekend. My family rarely did anything together except eat dinner a few times a week.

As a consequence, the dining room became the stage for our family dramas. Although my parents barely grumbled at each other, from time to time, I would catch one of them glancing furtively at the other. My eyes would dart back and forth anxiously from her to him, trying to decipher their body language and assess the toll of accumulated resentments. Back in those days, I didn't know a name for the discomfort I felt as I scrutinized my parents' interactions, flinching at the stiffness in their voices, the long tense silences. I never felt safe when they were together. The worry edged in on me and made my stomach ache.

In contrast, Vanessa, completely unfazed, talked non-stop. "I should have gotten the lead in the school play but the drama teacher Mr. Cartwright likes Erica Davis better so he gave her the lead role—it's so unfair—Dad you should call the principal and complain—I'm always the last one picked for the volleyball teams in gym even though I'm good in volleyball—I told the gym teacher I don't want to dress for gym anymore and she said I had to—everyone picks on me—I hate them all—I swear I'm going to find a way to get even—I wish we were Catholic and I could go to St. Joseph's and not the stupid public school with the stupid kids and stupid teachers. **I HATE ALL OF THEM!"**

"Vanessa, lower your voice. We're trying to eat dinner," my mother said, annoyed.

"WHO CARES!" Vanessa shouted back at her.

My parents looked at each other, my mother's eyes shooting silent daggers. When my father said nothing, my mother pushed her chair back from the table and walked up the stairs to her bedroom. Then the door slammed.

Vanessa, now completely agitated, turned to my father. "What's **HER** problem?" She threw her napkin on the table and ran up the stairs to her bedroom. Her door slammed.

My father and I looked at each other cautiously. "Well Grace, I guess we get to do the dishes," he said finally, forcing a faint smile.

"O.K. Daddy," I said, smiling back. I saw the now familiar look of worry on his face. As he rinsed the dishes, I watched his eyes, unfocused, staring off into space, tension wrinkling his forehead. The overhead kitchen light gave a reddish cast to his curly brown hair. I had often wished that, like Vanessa, I had my mother's pretty blond hair, but at that moment, I was happy to look like my father.

I was not surprised, the following morning, to see the neatly folded sheets and pillow stacked on the living room couch where my father had slept. I grabbed my school books and slipped out the back door, then walked to the corner where I waited for Vanessa to catch up.

Vanessa and I were walking home from school. I turned around. Suddenly she was gone. In a panic, I ran home. I felt in my pocket for the keys. They weren't there. I ran back and looked for her down the side streets. Then I was in a building, running from room to room, desperately searching. I called her name, again and again.

The next morning I woke up bleary-eyed and rattled by the dream. The whole day I chafed with worry that Vanessa would forget to wait for me after school.

*   *   *

By the time Vanessa reached the tenth grade, the gap in our ages seemed huge. I watched with fascination and envy as her body changed. The curve of her developing breasts, her narrowing waist, her long slim legs transformed her into a full-fledged teenager. I still had the body of a child, complete with scabs on my elbows and knees from roller-skating spills. I had always been a few inches shorter than Vanessa and couldn't imagine myself, with my skinny shapeless body, evolving as she had into a graceful, feminine figure.

She would stand in front of the bathroom mirror brushing her hair, meticulously applying her pink Sweet Sensation lip gloss, her eyeliner and mascara. She had a boyfriend now, Peter Vanelli, who would drive over in his father's bright red Chevrolet convertible to take her to the movies.

But mostly, high school proved to be a difficult time for Vanessa. One after another, her friendships ended badly. Molly McGann, whose older sister Maureen was Vanessa's age, told me that Vanessa had been dumped by the group of girls she was hanging out with. Three of them had spent weeks constructing a family tree of the Hapsburg Dynasty for a history class project. Vanessa and two other girls were working on their own project on Mussolini. She complained about it almost every night at dinner. She didn't like her partners, they weren't doing enough work. And the endless refrain—why couldn't she be on the Hapsburg team?

The research projects were to be presented in class the week before Christmas. The day before the presentation, Mr. Felker, Vanessa's history teacher, discovered all five poster boards containing the Hapsburg family tree doused with black ink. The project was ruined. The dean was brought in to investigate; even the principal showed up at the class to speak to the students.

A few weeks later, Vanessa was opening her locker when one of the girls, Penny Briggs, spotted a bottle of black printer's ink on the top shelf. She called down the hall to some of the other girls. Together, they nailed Vanessa on the spot. Maureen said Vanessa just kept shaking her head in a nervous flurry of denials. No one believed her. By the end of the day, the news had spread throughout the school. If not for Peter Vanelli, she would have been completely alone. The entire group of girls, all eight of them, refused to have anything more to do with her.

One night at dinner a few months later, my mother said, "Vanessa, Mrs. Mankowicz called me today." My father stopped eating, raising his eyes to look at my mother.

Vanessa dropped her fork and blurted, "Susie Mankowicz is a bitch! And a crybaby!" She and my mother, now both angry, glared tunneled beams of raw hatred at each other. Except for a thin scar on Vanessa's upper lip, gotten at age seven when she fell forward into a broken edge on her bicycle bell, they were mirror images of each other.

My mother stared at my father, her eyes flickering, indignant. "Tell your daughter . . ." She stopped, her breathing uneven, her fingers gripping the edge of the table.

"There is no cursing in this house!"

My father's voice piped in. "Finish what you started, Margaret. You're baiting her."

"I'm baiting her?" she said, shaking her head, twisting her napkin in both hands. "You know what—you're as crazy as she is!" She flung her napkin onto the table and ran up the stairs to her bedroom. The door slammed.

My father, his face blanched with anger, followed her, taking the steps two at a time. He banged on the door with enough force that I imagined his fists would split the wood.

"I'm not kidding, Margaret. Open the damn door!"

Still at the table, Vanessa and I, eyes wide with fear, looked at each other. I held my breath. I had never seen my father so enraged.

We could hear their shouting from behind the closed door, strident voices flinging hateful accusations.

First my mother, ". . . **she's spoiled rotten . . . . selfish . . . narcissistic . . .**"

Then my father, ". . . **you are constantly criticizing her . . .**"

"**The kids at school don't like her!**" My mother's voice rising to a shrill pitch. "**Even her counselor said so . . .**"

Vanessa's chair scraped the floor as she pushed back from the table. She stood up, put her hands over her ears and shouted, "**I HATE YOU!**" Then she turned and ran up the stairs to her own bedroom.

Alone at the table, I looked helplessly around the empty room, then jumped at the sudden blast from Vanessa's radio. With the volume on high, the sound of Blondie singing **Heart of Glass** made my mother's silver tea set rattle on the dining room breakfront. The shouting from my parents' bedroom suddenly stopped. Then the heavy thud of my father's footsteps running down the stairs. He went by me in a flash, to the kitchen and out the back door. Seconds later, his car started. I tiptoed to the window and watched him back down the driveway, wondering if I'd ever see him again.

I began clearing the table, putting away the uneaten food, washing the dishes. Vanessa and I often fought over doing the dishes, but now I was relieved to have something to do. I went up the stairs to my own bedroom, quietly closing the door. I sat shivering, staring out of my window to the street, to our neighbor, Mr. McKay, playing catch on the sidewalk with his son Gary while his wife stood watching from their front lawn. Had they heard the yelling? Did they argue during dinner? I turned on my radio and fell onto my bed, pressing my face into the pillow. The image of my father's face, white-hot with anger, thrashed around in my mind. I stayed awake until 11:30pm when, with relief, I heard him close the garage door.

A few days later, I spotted my father's Buick as Erin and I were leaving school. Vanessa, whose school dismissed a half-hour before mine, was sitting in the front passenger seat. What now? I thought. I grabbed Erin's arm and pulled her over to the car with me. "What's going on?" I asked my father. "Something bad happened, didn't it?"

"No, everything's fine. I was in the neighborhood and thought I'd take you and Vanessa for a coke."

"Can Erin come?" I asked, searching his face.

"Another time," he said quietly.

"It's okay, Grace," Erin whispered. "I'll see you tomorrow."

I turned and watched her walk away, then looked back at my father. "This isn't good, is it? I asked.

"It's okay, really. Everything's okay," he said.

Ten minutes later, the three of us were seated in a red vinyl booth at the Five Star Diner. Vanessa and I, next to each other, faced my father. I watched him as he stirred the milk in his coffee. Clearing his throat, he said quietly, "Your mother went to Chicago today to visit Uncle Will and Aunt Claire."

Uncle Will had married Aunt Claire about nine years earlier. Vanessa and I, ages eight and four at the time, had been flower girls at their wedding.

"Grammy will be staying with us. I want you both to help her fix dinner and do the dishes. Her arthritis—you know, it's hard for her."

"Is Mom coming back?" I burst in.

"Of course she is. She'll be back next week," he said.

"Are you sure?" I asked, feeling suddenly queasy.

"Yes, Grace. I'm sure."

Vanessa, who had been unusually quiet, said in a voice riddled with anger, "Well, I hope she stays there. I don't want her back." When I turned to look at her, I saw her flushed face and heard the familiar sound of teeth grinding.

* * *

Just before her 18th birthday, Vanessa left for college. Overnight, the noise level on Wentworth Street decreased dramatically, and a tentative peace settled into the house. I certainly didn't miss the fighting, the taunts, the awful scenes at dinner or the slamming doors. Even my parents spoke to each other in softer voices.

But I missed Vanessa. I longed for our ongoing games of monopoly, our walks to the mall, even our arguments.

My father stopped coming home for dinner at least two or three nights a week. He had opened his own civil engineering firm in the previous year and said he needed to take clients to dinner. My mother didn't seem to care. She had wandered off into her own life, volunteering at the community center and taking courses at Queens College to get a degree in social work. I was often the only one home and, for the most part, savored the peaceful solitude.

When Vanessa returned for an occasional weekend or school holiday, the old conflicts instantly flared. My mother would seethe over the attention my father gave to Vanessa. One night at dinner during Vanessa's Christmas break, my father asked her about her classes, her professors, her roommate, her grades. We were half-way through dessert when my mother suddenly turned to me and said, "We could be dead and they wouldn't notice."

My body stiffened, my fingers tightened around my water glass. Not only was she provoking an argument, she was insinuating me as her ally. I thought I knew what was coming next, but I turned out to be wrong in one significant detail. She pushed her chair back from the table, went to the hall closet where she got her coat and disappeared out the front door, instead of bounding up the stairs to her room, as I had expected.

I looked nervously at my father. His face had darkened, his eyes staring at the now vacant dining room chair. The sound of the slamming door was what finally silenced Vanessa. She had been talking non-stop, but she became strangely quiet. Then, gesturing with her fork in one hand, her knife in the other, she looked directly at my father and said, "I **HATE** her!" Her hands gripped the silverware. "It's always the **SAME FUCKING**

THING!" She looked down at her plate and shook her head violently. Her blond hair fell into her face.

I looked at my father, then at Vanessa, and took a slow, deep breath.

*   *   *

That was the year I started high school. On weekend afternoons, Erin and I walked for hours, wandering in and out of the shops on Main Street. One of our favorites, Tyson's Jewelers, sold inexpensive jewelry and drew in lots of teenagers. Two years earlier, we had gotten identical silver friendship rings there. We had the inside of mine engraved with Erin's name and hers with mine.

We'd meet Molly and Andrea at the Video Arcade where we took turns playing Ms Pacman. Between the arcade and the mall a few blocks away, we'd usually run into other kids from school. A bunch of us would meet on Friday nights at a school football or basketball game and afterwards would walk over to Swensons, the neighborhood ice cream parlor, or another hang-out, Hamburger Palace. If there wasn't a game, we went skating at Roller Heaven. On Friday nights, the place was packed with reckless teenagers zooming around the rink, loud rock music blaring through the speakers at excruciating decibels. They had a snack bar and a huge arcade with over twenty video game stations. One of us would stand in line to get quarters, feeding dollar bills into the change machine, while the rest of us reserved places at the games. We spent the whole week anticipating Friday nights.

On Saturday nights, both Erin and I had regular baby sitting jobs. Mine was with the Markhams, who lived around the corner from us. Their two little girls, Heather and Claudia, ages 6 and 4, would wait for me to walk up to their front door, their cute little faces pressed against the glass pane in their living room window. Both of them would run to the door to hug me when I walked in. Mrs. Markham was so pretty, with curly red hair which, sadly, neither of her daughters inherited. I still remember how Ruth Markham and her husband Ed smiled at each other. I wondered if my parents had ever looked at each other like that.

After Heather and Claudia went to bed, I'd wait for the Markhams to check in and, by 9 pm, I was on the phone with Erin. We had an endless array of topics to cover, the kids at school, the cute new twins (Billy and Bobby Foster), what to wear to the Halloween Dance, how to solve the last three problems in our algebra homework.

One particular Saturday afternoon, Erin and I had agreed to study together for a big biology test. We were on the phone making a plan when she heard Vanessa's voice in the background.

"I can't make it," Erin said suddenly.

I sensed she didn't like Vanessa but it was not something we talked about. "I'll go to your house, if you want." My offer was met with silence.

Then her response: "Grace . . . no. It's not a good idea. I can't . . . I'm not allowed to have friends over when my father's here."

Not allowed? I didn't know what to say. In all this time, I had seen Erin's father—a paunchy, balding man—only once, standing outside his station wagon one day after school. She never talked about him . . . or the rest of her family, for that matter. I guess I didn't think about it because I didn't talk about my family either.

Instantly, I regretted making the offer. I didn't even want to go there. With her five brothers and sisters, all younger, it was sometimes too noisy there to hear her on the phone.

"Then come here, please." My throat tightened. I tried to keep my voice even. Again silence. "What is it? Why won't you tell me?"

Slowly she picked out the words. She was uncomfortable around Vanessa. Vanessa intimidated her. She suspected Vanessa of stealing her earrings, little studs with jade stones. She had put them on my dresser the night of our sleepover those many years ago, and they weren't there in the morning.

I vaguely remembered seeing the earrings in Vanessa's jewelry box although I don't think she ever wore them. Because our bedrooms were opposite each other, I was able to watch Vanessa as I listened to Erin. I could see her sitting at her desk through the open door of my room. Her long blond hair was pulled together in a clip at the nape of her neck. I didn't recall ever seeing her wear her hair like this, but many years later, sitting next to her lawyer in a Manhattan courtroom, she had her hair pulled back in exactly the same way, fusing those two events together in my memory. When she turned, I saw the slight scar intersecting her upper lip, giving her mouth a barely perceptible tilt. I stared at her.

"Why didn't you tell me then?" I said quietly into the phone.

"How could I? What would I have said? That your sister's a thief?"

I couldn't answer her. Now there was silence on my end.

"I knew I shouldn't have told you," she said.

"I'm glad you told me. I wanted to know."

I hung up the phone. Sitting on my bed, I watched Vanessa at her desk. Then I got up and walked into her room. Lifting the cover of her jewelry box, I picked out the jade earrings. "Where did you get these?" I didn't take my eyes off her.

She looked at me innocently. "I traded earrings with Melanie Coleman. A long time ago." Her voice was cool and steady, without a hint of discomfort.

She said nothing as I dropped the earrings into my pocket. She didn't dare challenge me.

I returned to my room to call Erin. "Meet me in front of the library in an hour. Can you?"

She was already there when I arrived, sitting on the library steps, poking with a stick at something on the sidewalk, her red hair highlighted by the sun. I slipped the earrings into her pocket. "I'm sorry. I'm so sorry."

"I never blamed you," she said, smiling at me. When she squeezed my hand, I threw my arms around her and hugged her.

*   *   *

When summer came, Erin's family rented a cottage in upstate New York for the entire month of July. I felt completely bereft. My friends Andrea Jaeger and Molly McGann were also away, Andrea visiting her cousins in California for the summer and Molly working as a junior counselor at a sleep-away camp in New Hampshire. My days became impossibly long even though I worked three mornings a week in the town library. The librarian, Miss Zrinsky, had posted a job opening notice in the Guidance Office at school. Since Erin and I frequently used the library, Miss Zrinsky knew me and gave me the job. On Monday, Wednesday and Thursday mornings, I worked at the desk checking out books, shelving returns and cataloging periodicals.

I became very attached to Miss Zrinsky, a kind, middle-aged woman who, as a teenager, had emigrated from Poland. She had a slight trace of an accent and, from time to time, she switched the sounds of "v" and "w". So when Vanessa came to the library one Wednesday morning, Miss Zrinsky slipped and called her "Wanessa." I had to elbow Vanessa in the ribs to keep her from objecting.

Miss Zrinsky asked me all sorts of questions about myself. How did I spend my free time? What kind of books did I read? When I told her I had joined the school dance club, she took me to see the Joffrey Ballet. She gave me back issues of magazines, Seventeen and YM. In return, I took little gifts to her, a small milk glass vase with lilacs from the tree in our back yard, a green leather-covered calendar my father brought home from the office for me.

Having Vanessa home for July and August eased the boredom somewhat. We both had too much time on our hands and spent much of it together. Once or twice a week, I'd meet her at her job at the GAP, and we'd walk to the mall or go to a movie. For the first time, I began to challenge Vanessa's notion that she was entitled to control every plan, to make every decision. We argued about where to go, what movie to see. In retrospect, I believe that summer may have been the beginning of the end for us.

She rambled on endlessly about Timothy, her new boyfriend, who was working at a resort in the Colorado mountains for the summer. Timothy, who was tall and handsome, whose father owned three car dealerships on Long Island, whose family had a summer house in South Hampton, who was pursued by flocks of females but had chosen Vanessa. She wore his fraternity pin on her shirt and acted as if she were some kind of princess. She had the most annoying way of letting me know she thought my problems trivial. She actually laughed when I told her how much I missed Erin. "That's nothing, Grace. Just wait 'til you have a boyfriend. Missing Erin will seem like a joke." There were days I wished she would just go back to school. But we were both there and lonely; mutual need held us together.

One afternoon, we were sitting at the dining room table playing Hearts when my mother walked in. She looked at Vanessa and, eyeing the fraternity pin on her shirt, said, "Take that pin off the front of your blouse. It looks like you dribbled your dinner on it."

Looking intently at the cards she was holding, Vanessa leaned forward, taking a slow, deep breath. Her hair, combed to one side, fell forward on her face. "Bitch," she said, not quietly enough.

My mother's mouth curled into a sneer as she walked over to us. Vanessa jumped up, flashed a look of unmasked contempt at my mother and turned to leave. Grabbing her shirt, my mother swung Vanessa around and, from across the table, I felt the force of her open hand against Vanessa's face. Vanessa, mouth agape, put her hand against the growing red splotch on her cheek.

I jumped up. "Mom! Stop!" I shouted at her.

She shot an angry look in my direction, then bolted up the stairs. Her bedroom door slammed, the lock clicked. Seconds later, Vanessa was on the stairs. Her door slammed.

Stunned, I looked at the cards in disarray on the table. I put my face in my hands and tried to steady my breathing. After a few minutes, I slipped my keys into my pocket and walked over to a neighborhood park where my father used to take us to play on the tire swings. I sank down into a mound of uncut grass, wrapping my arms around my waist to ease the ache in my stomach.

I couldn't erase the image of my mother lashing out at Vanessa. It made me think about a conversation I'd overheard years ago when my mother confessed to Uncle Will her fear that she had inherited their father's personality. I later learned that my grandfather, Howard Gilman, had been wounded during World War II and had subsequently become an alcoholic. Three surgeries failed to correct the nerve damage caused by shrapnel buried in his left arm. It hung limp at his side.

He became a frustrated, angry drunk. At first, he only hit his wife, Pauline, but eventually he went after his three children as well. One good arm was all he needed.

My Uncle Chris drew the worst of it. By the age of eight, he had developed a tic, an involuntary spasm that raked across his face, jerking his left eye shut. Then he began stuttering. Uncle Will got stomach aches which eventually escalated into chronic digestive problems by his mid-thirties. My mother clenched her teeth with enough force that, by the time she was a teenager, she needed pain killers to soothe the ache in her jaw.

I never met my Uncle Chris. On those infrequent occasions his name was mentioned, my mother's eyes widened with startled surprise. If someone asked her about him, she'd shrug. She kept a few pictures of him in her top dresser drawer. More than once, Vanessa and I peeked in there to look. In one, he was standing between my mother and Will in front of their house, his chin jutting forward awkwardly. On the back of the photo, written in pencil—Margaret 10, Chris 8, Will 6. The other picture was of Chris in his army uniform, alone and unsmiling, the day before he left for Viet Nam.

In the same drawer, buried under a stack of letters and a box of jewelry, was a picture of my grandparents, whom I had also never met. It was one of those old black and white photos, faded and torn almost in half, patched tenuously together by a piece of yellowed scotch tape. A thin, frail woman, Pauline looked dwarfed next to her hulking bear of a husband. Howard's large size accentuated his injured arm, shriveled and dangling at his side.

I stood up, brushing the leaves off my shorts and headed toward the library. I wondered why my mother wasn't nicer to Vanessa since she knew how it felt to be treated badly. It didn't make sense.

Ten minutes later, I poked my head into Miss Zrinsky's office at the back of the reading room. She was at her desk, her fingers nimble on her old Smith Corona typewriter. She never used the word processor which sat covered in a far corner on an old metal table.

"Grace?" she said, looking at her watch. "I wasn't expecting you until tomorrow morning."

"I just felt like coming over."

"Well, come on in," she said, smiling. "You can help me put labels on the new filmstrips."

After she typed the labels, I smeared them with glue and pressed them onto the metal filmstrip containers. Gratefully, I spent the rest of the afternoon there.

"Miss Zrinsky, do you have children?" I asked.

"No, Grace, I don't. I was never married. I guess it wasn't in my cards. Is that how you say it?"

I smiled at her. "Yes, that's how you say it."

That night, another dream, an unwelcome intruder:

I walked over to the library but it wasn't there. In its place were brick houses, similar to our house on Wentworth Street. I kept walking. Up ahead, I saw the library in the next block. I ran to it and pushed the front door open. There was my mother—sitting behind the counter in Miss Zrinsky's chair.

*   *   *

Mercifully, the summer ended. Erin and I returned to school, now in the tenth grade. I told Miss Zrinsky I would take fewer hours if she hired both of us. So, we each worked two afternoons a week, with Tuesdays in common.

Miss Zrinsky's generosity enveloped us. She helped me find the resource materials I needed for a history paper on the Battle of Yorktown and gave Erin ideas for her book report on **Great Expectations**. She cut out a series of New York Times articles on choosing a college and put them in a file for us. One Saturday afternoon, she took us to a book fair, showing us how to take the subway into Manhattan.

After that, we went into Manhattan whenever we could. Miss Zrinsky gave us free passes to the dinosaur exhibit at the Museum of Natural History and took us to an open-air concert at the South Street Seaport. She got us a subway map and circled the stations we could use to catch the E train back to Queens.

When she invited us to a production of **The Nutcracker** at Lincoln Center, Erin said, "We can't, Miss Zrinsky. You've already done too much for us."

"You are the daughters I never had," she said.

And you are the mother I never had, I thought to myself.

*   *   *

One Sunday in May, Erin and I went into the city and spent most of the afternoon wandering the length of the crowded Third Avenue Street Fair. Block after block, folding tables displayed wares of one sort or another. Clothing, make-up, toys, jewelry, pots and pans, pillows and towels, reading glasses, sunglasses, batteries, food from at least a dozen different countries. Like little kids, we ran from table to table to survey the goods. After several blocks of browsing, Erin stopped at a vendor to look at some earrings while I continued down the street to buy us a coke. As I started to make my way back to her, I saw her from a distance holding a mirror, her head tilted to one side. I could see her freckles even from a half-block away. With her left hand, she held her hair back to look at the earrings. As I got closer, she turned abruptly and stared at me, the color suddenly draining from her face. She quickly took off the earrings and rushed over to me.

"What's the matter?" I asked.

She shook her head and pushed me backwards, spilling the coke all over my arm.

"Erin, what's wrong?" I turned to look for some napkins when I saw him. The muscles in my chest tightened and I gulped in a mouthful of air. Several feet behind Erin was my father, arm-in-arm with a woman, a very pretty woman with black hair and dark brown eyes. They were looking at each other and laughing. For one very long moment. When he saw me, the smile on his face evaporated instantly. He stared at me and I could see he was holding his breath.

I stood absolutely still, staring back at him . . . at them. My right eyelid started to twitch. I pressed my hand against it. No one spoke. No one even moved. Finally, not knowing what else to do, I turned and walked away. Erin was next to me, clutching my arm. I let myself lean against her. He didn't follow us.

We walked five blocks to the subway without speaking. On the train, I felt frozen, a lump of lifeless salt, barely moving, staring at nothing. Erin tugged gently on my arm when we arrived at our stop. We climbed the stairs to the street and continued walking. Tears burned behind my eyelids. Why was I surprised? Had anything changed? Would he leave us now for good?

Erin walked me home, holding my hand. Neither one of us knew what to say. I saw tears on her cheek and gave her a hug before I went into the house. Hours later, I heard my father's car pull into the driveway. I got up quickly and pushed my bedroom door closed. Sick with nauseating dread, I waited for the knock on my door. It never came.

Several days passed before I saw him since he'd left on a business trip the following morning. He walked into the kitchen just as I was pouring myself some orange juice. I looked at him squarely, eyeball to eyeball. He opened his mouth to speak but nothing came out. Enough time had passed to allow my anxiety and dread to dissipate. Now I was angry. I turned my back to him and walked into my bedroom. This time he followed me.

"Grace . . . I . . ." Then silence. Without looking at him, I started folding the two sweaters I had thrown on the chair. I could feel him watching me. Then his voice, "I'm sorry, Grace."

I didn't respond. I had been schooled in the silent treatment by a master.

"Say something, Grace." His voice was hoarse and unnaturally stiff.

I saw the worry lines etched in his forehead. Still I said nothing. He couldn't make me talk. Never before had I felt such power.

"This situation . . ." He cleared his throat.

I looked at the web of wrinkles around his eyes. He looked suddenly tired . . . and older than I knew he was.

"You know, your mother and I . . ." He stopped, shaking his head. "We haven't been happy together."

Really, Dad. Did you think I hadn't noticed? I said nothing. I crossed my arms in front of my chest. The pose reminded me of my mother. Quickly, I let them fall. I shifted my feet. I was losing the edge. In an instant, my eyes brimmed with tears. He saw them and started toward me. I held up my hand to stop him. He stopped.

"Grace. . . . I'm sorry you're upset." His voice, lacking its usual confident authority, seemed unfamiliar.

"You didn't even come to my bedroom to find me," I blurted out. I wanted to say more but I was now sobbing.

He put his arms around me. I heard him whispering but the words were inaudible. I let myself cry. He continued to hold me. When I was done, he kissed the top of my head and slipped quietly out of the room.

Later that evening, for reasons I still do not understand, I called Vanessa in her dorm room and told her the story. She gasped, then declared with authority, "I'm not surprised."

Typical Vanessa. Always one up on the rest of us.

*　　*　　*

Months passed. The air in our house pulsated, thick with strained silence. I watched my father, now sleeping in Vanessa's bed, waiting for some sign telegraphing his intention to leave. When he stayed out late, I kept myself awake until I heard his car tires crunching the on bluestone driveway. I didn't know how to tell him I needed him. What would happen when Vanessa came home? My mother couldn't be counted on to hold things together. To hold us together.

In the end, he didn't leave, at least not then. The three of us continued the charade, some evenings eating dinner together like other normal families. Our conversations, if you could call them conversations, were measured and cautious. The weather, a headline in the news, a housewares sale at Macy's, please pass the meatloaf. Three quiet voices trying not to upset the fragile balance.

I had to remind myself that my mother didn't know about the pretty, dark-haired woman. At least, I don't think she did.

What did it matter anyway? As far as I could see, she showed no interest in anything my father did.

One evening while I was doing my homework, I heard my parents talking, their voices rising suddenly through the hall outside my bedroom. I tiptoed to the bathroom to get closer, straining to make out their words, muffled behind the closed door. Afraid they would hear me, I didn't move to get any closer.

For several nights, these muted conversations continued but never loud enough to be understandable. A few days later, my mother was peeling potatoes at the kitchen sink when I got home from school.

"Mom . . . ." I said, cautiously. "What's going on? I hear you and Dad . . . um . . . arguing every night."

She turned to look at me and, in that moment, I remember thinking she had a prettier face than the dark-haired woman at the street fair.

"Vanessa's having some problems at school," she said, scraping at the potato skins.

"What kind of problems?"

"You know, Grace. I probably shouldn't say any more than that right now." With the back of her hand, she pushed some hair off her face and began slicing the potatoes.

"I knew you wouldn't tell me." I shook my head in disgust, pushing my way through the swinging kitchen door and up to my bedroom. Tempted to slam my door, I instead flipped on my boom box. Van Halen singing **Jump**—my mother hated that music. I reached over and turned up the volume. Fifteen minutes later, she walked in and handed me a letter. She watched as I read it.

Dear Mr.& Mrs. Strickland:

It is with sincere regret that I apprise you of accusations made by another student against your daughter, Vanessa Strickland.

An investigation conducted by the University has substantiated a number of his allegations involving breaking-and-entering and the destruction of property.

The University has scheduled a hearing on Tuesday, November 13th at 1:00 p.m. in my office, Room 112 in the Administration Building. You are strongly encouraged to attend. Although the hearing has no official legal status, you may bring an attorney if you wish.

Feel free to contact me if you require additional information.

Yours truly,
John P. Stanton
Dean of Students

My mouth dropped open. I raised my eyes to look at my mother. "What does this mean? What other student?" I stopped to catch my breath. Breaking-and-entering? Oh, Vanessa.

"Her boyfriend. Ex-boyfriend now," my mother said.

"What did she do?" My voice agitated, trembling.

"He says he broke up with her. He took his pin back. A week later, he was walking down the street, holding hands with another girl when he ran into Vanessa. A few days after that someone went into his dorm room and cut up his clothes. With a pinking shears."

Oh my god. The pinking shears.

"They say they have proof it was Vanessa," my mother said, shaking her head.

*　　*　　*

On the morning of November 13, my parents made the five-hour drive to the University of Buffalo. They called later that day to tell me to spend the night at my grandmother's.

Grammy, as we still called her, was sitting in her favorite arm chair working on her needlepoint when I got there. She motioned to the plate of freshly baked oatmeal cookies sitting on the coffee table.

"I hope Vanessa's feeling better," she said.

Did she know? "Uh . . . what do you mean, Grammy?" I asked.

"Your mother told me Vanessa's been in the infirmary with the flu. Isn't that why they were driving up there?" She squinted at me over the top of her reading glasses, as if waiting for verification.

"Oh . . . yes . . . well, everything's probably okay," I said quickly.

Changing the subject, I motioned toward her needlepoint. "Gram, what are you making?"

"A wall-hanging. For Elyse's new office."

"I talked to Aunt Elyse last week," I said. "She told me she likes her new job in Philadelphia. You must miss her a lot."

My grandmother nodded, sighing. "I'm taking a train to Philadelphia next month. Elyse invited me for the weekend. I hope to finish this needlepoint in time. Maybe you'll help me pick out a frame."

"Sure. That'll be fun. We haven't been shopping together in a long time. And there's a frame shop near here, over on Bell Boulevard. I can meet you one day after school."

*   *   *

The following evening my parents returned with Vanessa and all of her belongings. I was standing in the foyer when she walked in. She ran past me up the stairs to her bedroom without a glance in my direction.

She had been suspended for the rest of the semester. She would be permitted to return on probation after the Christmas holiday break when she'd be able to take her final exams, on the condition that she get counseling.

The next day Vanessa went over to the GAP to apply for a job. I only know this because I saw her there through the store window when Erin, Andrea and I walked past it after school. I quickly crossed to the other side of the street, hoping she wouldn't see us and want to come along. I had already spent too many years in her outsized shadow and didn't want her encroaching on my new life.

It turned out to be a needless worry. Vanessa showed no interest in me or my friends. Between her work hours and my school schedule, we seldom saw each other. I began to wonder if she was deliberately avoiding me.

At dinner, she was surprisingly reserved, cautious even, particularly around my mother. I didn't know how to react to this startling change in her. In the past, I always had to struggle against her dominance, especially at the dinner table when she had typically commandeered almost every conversation. Now she seemed to have folded into herself. It unsettled me.

After a few nights, I knocked on her bedroom door. From inside, I heard the muted response, "I'm busy."

Gently, I pushed against the door and walked in. She swiveled around in her chair to look at me, her eyes red and puffy.

"Vanessa," I whispered. "Do you want to talk?"

She sat there, saying nothing, staring at the floor. Suddenly her face twisted into a pained grimace and her shoulders shook with sobs. I walked over to her and put my arms around her. Still sitting, she wrapped her arms around my waist, pressed her face into the front of my shirt and cried. When she stopped, I handed her the box of kleenex from her dresser. She wiped her eyes, blew her nose and let the crumpled wads of tissue fall to the floor.

Finally, in a thin, faltering voice, she said, "My life is a mess. I don't know what to do."

I sat down on the edge of her bed and reached for her hand, trying to figure out something to say.

"Do you believe he dumped me? He dumped me and I'm the one who gets suspended! This is so wrong." She shook her head, her cheeks streaked with tears.

I wanted to ask what exactly she thought was so wrong, but I knew the question would rankle her. "Maybe you should go somewhere else, Vanessa. You know . . . get a fresh start at a different college."

"No!" Her response emphatic, angry. "I don't **want** to go anywhere else. **He** should go somewhere else."

*   *   *

Vanessa's counseling sessions lasted two weeks. I overheard my father encouraging her to continue, but she wouldn't budge. At least he convinced her not to return to Buffalo, worried as he was about her running into Timothy and having to deal with the inevitable campus gossip. So in January, the two of them drove to register her at Hartwick College, a small school in Oneonta, not far from Albany.

Things did not go well for Vanessa at Hartwick. The first visible sign appeared with her mid-term grades. Two C's, two D's and an F. I overheard my parents arguing about her almost nightly.

My mother advocated for pulling the plug on Vanessa who, in her view, had squandered one opportunity after another. The expense of college burdened all of us, as she put it—a transparent ruse, I thought, to disguise what seemed like an unquenchable desire to make Vanessa suffer. She should come home and work. She should pay her own way.

That's all we need, I thought . . . to have Vanessa back here full time.

Predictably, my father defended Vanessa. She had been through a humiliating ordeal and needed time to adjust to her new environment. Now more than ever, she needed their support.

Nightly phone calls were made to Vanessa in her dorm room. My father offered assistance, my mother issued warnings. Vanessa promised to do better.

A few weeks later, she called me. From the tremulous sound in her voice, I could hear her struggling, trying to hold herself together.

"What's wrong?" I asked.

"I don't want to be here anymore." She was almost whispering.

"But you just got there a few months ago," I said.

Silence.

"Grace, listen. Would you come up here for a weekend? This weekend?"

I hesitated, knowing it would mean missing Molly McGann's party on Saturday night.

"You could tell Mom and Dad you want to see Hartwick," she went on.

"I'm not sure I can. I mean . . . not this weekend."

"Grace . . . . please come," she said, her voice cracking. "God . . . when have I **ever** asked . . . I **need** you to come."

"Okay." I caved in because it was true—she had never asked me for anything.

Three days later, I pulled my duffle bag onto a Greyhound bus headed for Oneonta. Vanessa was waiting at the terminal when I arrived. Substantially thinner even since Christmas, her face looked gaunt, tight, her eyelids heavy. And her hair, that beautiful blond hair, stringy and uncombed. Her hands fidgeted with the strap on her shoulder bag. She put on her sunglasses; her lower lip quivered. In less than two months, she had morphed into some unrecognizable being. I waited for her to say something but she simply motioned toward a waiting taxi. We traveled to her dorm in silence.

"Vanessa, what's going on?" I asked, finally.

She cleared her throat. "Things aren't . . . going very well," she said lamely, her voice breaking. Then she stopped talking. When the taxi pulled up to the dorm, she busied herself extracting bills from her wallet. After she paid the driver, I followed her up to the second floor.

I looked around her room, not even half the size of our bedrooms on Wentworth Street. The furniture, jammed into the small space, over-filled the room. A twin bed, a desk, a dresser and a two-shelf book case—everything in drab, institutional beige. The walls, also beige, were completely bare except for a large rectangular-shaped bulletin board hanging over the desk.

A silver thumb tack held in place a single scrap of paper. I walked over to it and saw a phone number written in pencil. I turned back to Vanessa. "What happened to your roommate?" I asked.

She wiped her eyes with the back of her hand. "She got on my nerves. I moved into this single two weeks ago."

"Do Mom and Dad know?" I was surprised I hadn't heard about her moving.

"Dad knows. I don't know if he told Mom. What does it matter anyway?" Her voice trailed off. She slumped down on the bed and covered her face with her hands.

"Tell me what's happening," I said, leaning against the book case facing her. She walked to her desk and retrieved an envelope from the drawer. Without a word, she handed it to me.

Smith, Williams & Wahl
Attorneys-at-Law

April 29, 1984

Dear Miss Strickland:

My office has confirmed that, since January 9th of this year, in excess of 120 phone calls have been made from your telephone to that of my client, Timothy Hamer. Of these calls, 79 have occurred between the hours of 12:00 a.m. to 5:00 a.m. Your intention to cause maximum disruption is clear.

I have advised Mr. Hamer to file a complaint of harassment with the local police in the event that these calls do not stop immediately.

If the calls continue, we will turn the matter over to the police. We will also send a copy of this letter to officials at Hartwick College.

I strongly encourage you to take notice of this warning.

Yours truly,

Stephen B. Wahl, Esquire

I raised my eyes from the letter to Vanessa. "You made all these calls?" I whispered. "One hundred and twenty phone calls?" I couldn't even imagine it.

"Well he deserved it. It was his fault," Vanessa snapped. She stopped to catch her breath. "He made promises to me. And I believed him." She glared at me, shouting, "**HE HUMILIATED ME!**" She put her hands over her ears and shook her head. Then, "I had to leave Buffalo . . . the college I should be graduating from. Because of him."

"I think you had to leave because you cut up his clothes," I said quietly.

"My god, Grace. You're defending him!"

She tore up a piece of paper she'd been clutching, her hands shaking.

"No, no. I'm not. Of course, I'm not," I said quickly.

She didn't respond. She sat on the edge of her bed, staring off at nothing, picking at her already mutilated cuticles. After a few minutes, I broke the silence.

"Vanessa, what do you want to do?"

She shrugged. "I want this whole thing to just go away," she said. Her lower lip was trembling again, her body slack, defeated.

"Then let it. Let it go away. They won't do anything if you stop."

She continued to sit, now staring out the window and said nothing.

"Vanessa," I said. "I get the feeling there's more . . ." My voice was louder than I meant it to be. "Tell me the rest of it," I said, lowering my voice.

"I kept calling. I couldn't stop. I tried . . ." Her voice trailed off. I watched a tear drop from her lower lash onto her cheek.

"And then what?" I asked.

Silence.

"Vanessa, why are you making me drag this out of you?" I struggled to keep the frustration out of my voice.

She began again. "Last week, I got a summons to appear in court. On September 18." Her voice, barely audible, had dropped to a near whisper. "How am I going to get to Buffalo without Mom and Dad knowing?"

I saw the anxiety in her face, her eyes wide, her teeth biting into her lower lip. I started to say something but she waved me off.

"Now the dean here wants to see me. They sent a copy of the police report to the dean," her voice rising again. "I swear to god, he's trying to RUIN my life. Isn't it bad enough he dumped me?" She was shouting now, her hands balled into fists. "Then he files a police report. I can't believe it." She started to cry, her arms crossed in front and wrapped around her waist. She began rocking, forward and back.

I took a deep breath. Suddenly my head hurt. I pressed my finger tips into my forehead. I wanted to make her see—it seemed so obvious.

"Vanessa . . ." I said softly. "Maybe he's not trying to ruin your life. Maybe he thinks you're trying to ruin his life."

"Who cares what he thinks!" she snapped back. "He started it."

"Okay. He started it, but the only way this can end is if you stop calling him." I was now kneeling in front of her, holding her hands.

"What about him?" she demanded, pushing my hands away. Her eyes, blazing with anger, stared laser-like into mine. She grit her teeth as she grabbed my arms. "What about all the things he's done to me?"

I wanted to shake her and yell at her to stop. I didn't know how to get through to her. As I sat and watched her shoulders convulse with sobs, I felt a sting in my own eyes. Life had boomeranged on Vanessa and somehow she'd become her own worst enemy. I knew I was there because she didn't have anyone else to call.

*   *   *

Leaving Oneonta Sunday afternoon brought me no relief. I thought of nothing but Vanessa during the interminable bus ride. Images of her in escalating states of hysteria played and replayed in my mind. What would she do? Would she keep calling him? Would she go to Buffalo and attack him with her pinking shears? Would she hurt herself?

The next day in school, too agitated to concentrate, I ran out after my last class. I put a hurried note on Erin's locker and walked over to the library. I found Miss Zrinsky in the back office.

"Grace?" She looked at me closely. "Did something happen?"

Dropping my book bag on the floor, I collapsed into the chair in front of her. "Oh Miss Zrinsky . . ." The tears spilled down my face. I wiped them away with the sleeve of my sweater and told her about Vanessa.

Miss Zrinsky reached over, putting her hand on my arm. "Do your parents know?" she asked, her eyes intense with concern.

I shook my head. "I promised Vanessa I wouldn't tell. I don't want to tell them. I want to be a million miles from here when they find out."

"Grace, your parents should know. Maybe they can help Vanessa. This is too much for you."

I knew she was right, but I shuddered at the idea of telling them. So I waited . . . while the weeks passed.

I'm not even sure how the story reached them, but when it happened, they were consumed by it. At night from my bedroom, I could hear the endless arguing. Nothing, not even my loudest music, obliterated those sounds.

Summer vacation was a week away. I dreaded Vanessa's return and the inevitable fighting between her and my mother. When my own school year ended, I stayed out of the house as much as possible. In the mornings, I worked as a counselor in a local day camp and, three afternoons a week, in the library with Miss Zrinsky. Erin was away with her family, but Molly and Andrea were around. The three of us depended on each other to fill the long summer days.

Vanessa worked full-time at The GAP, including weekends and some evenings. The three nights she didn't work, the family dinners in our house became tension-filled, painful events. My grandmother's arrival on Sunday nights provided the only reprieve, when the slightest sign of discord summoned an instantaneous look of reproof from my father.

Vanessa's presence triggered a deeply-held mean streak in my mother, who harped ad nauseum about the September 18 court date. "I hope you're putting money aside for the trip to Buffalo. It's time you started paying for the trouble you cause."

"Margaret," my father cut her off. "Just leave her alone."

"Don't blame me. I'm not responsible for any of this." She glared at him with disgust.

But most of the time we ate in guarded silence. The clatter of forks scraping against the porcelain plates was often the only sound in the room.

*   *   *

Most weekends, Andrea, Molly and I took the train out to Rockaway Beach. We would lay our beach towels next to one another's, securing the corners with our sandals. Then we'd turn on Molly's new boom box and take turns slathering Coppertone on each other's backs. The beach was always crowded with kids our age, some we knew, many we did not.

Early in July, Andrea met Mike Jenkins at the hot dog stand and brought him over to meet us. He left and returned with three friends, Doug, Larry and Lenny. Like us, they were 16 and went to a high school about eight miles from our own. Soon the seven of us started meeting at the beach. One rainy Saturday, we met them at a movie on Queens Boulevard, mid-way between our two neighborhoods.

We sat in the last row eating popcorn, watching **Back to the Future**. Near the end of the movie, Lenny, seated next to me, leaned over and kissed me. I felt a flutter in my chest, a wave of giddiness. He squeezed my hand. I put my head on his shoulder, breathing in the aroma of his Old Spice.

Now I had a new, urgent reason to look forward to the weekends. The next Tuesday, I dragged Andrea and Molly to Macy's to buy a new bathing suit. I picked out a black bikini, sexy and sophisticated next to the red and white polka dotted one-piece I'd been wearing. By Wednesday, I was fully distracted with excitement and anticipation. Thursday afternoon, Miss Zrinsky gave me a quizzical look as she motioned me over to the front desk. I had mis-filed the check-out cards, putting the C's into the section with the P's.

Saturday morning, on the train to Rockaway, my excitement dissolved into stomach-churning doubt. I hadn't spoken to Lenny all week. Did he have my phone number? I couldn't remember. Had he changed his mind?

After we got to the beach, I saw the four of them sprawled out on their towels behind the third life guard stand, our favorite spot. When

Lenny looked at me with a shy, embarrassed smile, I realized he must be as nervous as I was. I kicked off my sandals and let myself flop down on the towel next to him. Then he took a handful of sand and sprinkled it on my toes as I giggled with relief.

He was my Saturday afternoon boyfriend for the rest of the summer. After Labor Day weekend, I never saw him again though we spoke on the phone from time to time. But the scent of Old Spice still transports me back to memories of my summer at Rockaway beach with Lenny Paulson.

*   *   *

Erin came home at the end of August. We met in front of the library, throwing our arms around each other, laughing and hugging. She looked beautiful to me, her hair bleached to auburn by the sun, her face and arms dotted with freckles.

We walked to the park behind our old junior high school, sat in the grass and talked about the summer. Erin had worked at a Dairy Queen not far from the cottage where her family stayed, swirling the ice cream from those big silver machines into cones and sundaes. She had learned how to water ski and strum chords on the guitar, which she brought along to show me. She held out her arm so I could see the thin raw-hide bracelet she had gotten from Greg Wilson, a counselor at a nearby sleep-away camp. A few nights a week, some of the counselors would drive into town to get sundaes at the Dairy Queen where Erin worked. Greg started hanging around the counter, flirting with her. Soon they were meeting on his day off, at the town square next to the red, white and blue tourist information booth.

I told her about Andrea and Molly and our weekends at the beach and, of course, about Lenny Paulson.

We walked over to Main Street, to the make-up counters at Macy's, trying on the different shades of lip gloss and eye-liner. From there, we went to J Crew and each bought a sweater and pair of jeans, then to the library to see Miss Zrinsky and negotiate our work schedules for the fall. I was relieved to have the summer behind me . . . to have Erin back.

*   *   *

Late in August, Vanessa left for Hartwick, returning a few weeks later for her court appearance. My father met her at the bus and the two of them drove to Buffalo that same night. The next day after school, I spent an extra hour in the library with Miss Zrinsky. As it turned out, my mother wasn't even home when I got there. The house was unexpectedly quiet and peaceful.

Vanessa and my father returned just before 9 o'clock. From my bedroom, I heard my mother's voice. I tiptoed into the hall.

"What happened?" she asked them. There was no response. Then louder, "I said what happened?"

"It's over, Margaret. Let it go." My father's voice, full of authority.

"Oh. So the two of you have decided to shut me out. I should've expected it."

She turned her back to them and walked out of the room. I was one floor above her, crouched behind the railing on the stairs. In the foyer, she turned suddenly and spat the words at Vanessa, "They should have sent you to jail." Her face, red and contorted, was nearly unrecognizable. I swallowed hard and looked away.

"They should send **YOU** to hell!" Vanessa screamed back, gesturing wildly. "**YOU HATEFUL DISGUSTING WITCH!**" Her entire body was trembling, her right eye blinking rapidly. It made me think of my Uncle Chris and his tic.

I held my breath, my heart thumping.

My mother's face drained to the color of flour. She wheeled around toward my father, who was still standing in the living room. His mouth seemed to be frozen open.

"This is the monster you created!" she hissed at him, her voice like a steam leak. "You don't care how she talks to me!" She stopped to catch her breath. "Don't expect anything from me . . . **NOT EVER AGAIN!**"

"He doesn't **WANT** anything from you!" Vanessa took a step toward my mother. For a crazed second, I thought Vanessa might hit her. **"HE'S HAD ANOTHER WOMAN FOR YEARS."** She said each word slowly, with enunciated precision.

They glared stark hatred at each other. Upstairs, clutching the railing, I barely managed to breathe. Blood pounded in my head. My mother raised her hand to her mouth, then ran from the room.

"Why don't you slam a few doors on your way!" Vanessa shouted after her.

I closed my eyes, my fingers stiff from gripping the banister.

*   *   *

The rest unraveled with lightning speed. The next day Vanessa was gone by the time I got home from school. My father slept on the couch for five nights; then he was gone. It was as if half my family had been plucked away . . . in less than a week.

Several days after he left, I saw my father standing outside his blue Buick, waiting for me as Erin and I were leaving school. I told Erin to go on without me and walked over to him.

He put his arm around me. "Are you okay?" he asked.

I nodded.

"Good. Let's go somewhere. I'll buy you a coke."

We got into his car. "How's your mother?" he asked.

I shrugged. "Fine, I guess." Then, "Are you coming back?"

He pulled the visor down to block the sun and, without looking at me, said, "No, Grace. I'm not."

"It was a stupid question." I looked out the passenger window.

For a minute, neither of us spoke. "Grace, I'm sorry for the way things have been. I know you often got the short end." He hesitated. Then abruptly, "I want you to come and live with me."

"You want me to leave her, too?" I asked.

He looked startled, surprised perhaps by my bluntness. "I want you to know you're not stuck there. Not if you don't want to be."

"Is Vanessa with you?" I asked.

"No. She's at school."

"Is your friend . . . I mean . . . that woman . . . is she with you?" Blushing suddenly, I looked down at the book bag in my lap. She had never before been mentioned by either of us.

"Her name is Valerie, Grace. She's there some of the time."

I felt his eyes on me. The back of my neck burned with heat.

We sat there for several minutes, not speaking. Thoughts raced through my mind, of my mother alone, of the dark-haired woman—now with a name—who seemed to have chiseled a permanent place in my father's life. I didn't know what to say.

"I don't know," I said quietly. "I can't think right now."

"You don't need to decide now. Tell me whenever you want. I just want you to know you can count on me. No matter what."

I was seventeen years old. It was the longest conversation we had ever had.

* * *

When I think back on those months alone with my mother, I'm amazed at how remarkably serene they were. The shouting, the bitter arguments, the door slamming—all of it gone. We floated into an easy comfortable space.

The change in my mother appeared almost immediately, the new softness in her voice, the tightness gone from her face. She looked like she had in the picture with my father, the one on the shelf in the living room wall unit, she standing in front of him grinning, he with arms around her, his cheek against her hair.

When she didn't have school, we ate together at the kitchen table, talking about the small things that filled our days. She told me about her classes, the Group Dynamics course, her favorite, and one of the new families at the community center who had lost a son to leukemia. Tears pooled above her lower lashes as she described the young, grieving mother of the boy. How odd that she had become so involved with this family. It was a side of her completely unknown to me.

One night at dinner, I took advantage of our new-found rapport and asked her what happened to my Uncle Chris. She sat for a long time without speaking, twisting her napkin in her hands. Finally, she brought it to her face and wiped the corners of her mouth. "Chris was so afraid of my father . . . it took over his life. He stuttered, his face twitched. I can still close my eyes and see the tremble in his lower lip. And the tic, that god awful tic smack in the middle of his face. The kids at school made fun of him. He had nowhere to go. Not school. Not home. It was terrible."

"Couldn't anyone help him?" I remembered one of the photos I had seen of Chris as a kid, his skinny arms hanging at his side, his upper teeth biting his lower lip.

"Not really," she said. "I mean . . . who could've helped him? My mother was so weak and pathetic. Will and I were just kids." She took a deep breath, frown lines creasing her forehead.

"What happened to Chris?"

She shook her head and sighed heavily. "He dropped out of high school and worked for awhile in a paint factory, then in some giant hardware outlet. A string of jobs leading nowhere. Eventually he joined the army and went to Viet Nam. The United States had started sending troops there. That was before the real bad fighting began. About five years later, he sent me a postcard from Thailand. I never heard from him after that. Will tried to find him. He got in touch with the army and was told Chris had been discharged."

"How come you never talk about your parents?" I asked.

She closed her eyes. "I try not to think about them," she said. "They were both so . . ." She looked over at me. "Inadequate. Fundamentally inadequate."

Years later, I repeated that phrase to Vanessa, who pointed her index finger, like a gun, and said, "Bingo. An apt description of Margaret, if I ever heard one."

I censored the small voice stuck in my throat that wanted to ask her why she hadn't done better as a parent. Instead, I pressed her about my grandparents. "Tell me about them . . . please."

She shook her head.

"Please."

She looked at me and our eyes locked. "My father came home from the Pacific front when I was two. He had enlisted when the Japanese attacked Pearl Harbor. Anyway, he was wounded and lost the use of his left arm. He got a job in a factory near the Brooklyn Navy Yard. Since we lived in Queens, his commute took more than an hour each way. He'd come home angry and frustrated. I've never forgotten the night he threw a book at my mother, yelling, 'You take two subways and a bus to some goddamn factory and try meeting your quota with one goddamn arm!' The boys and I hid in the pantry. All three of us were paralyzed with fear."

I took a slow, deep breath. "What'd your mother do?"

"My mother? Oh god, Grace. She just took it. Sometimes I think I should've been more charitable toward her because my father often came home drunk and he hit her . . . a lot. But she did nothing. She was meek and passive—she'd make these small fearful gestures that made me want to scream at her. I swear she would've faded into the beige walls if she had known how."

"It sounds pretty awful for her," I said quietly.

She shrugged. "I guess. But when he started hitting us and we'd run to her for protection, all we ever got was some numbed, deadened stare. Just looking at her made me cringe. And it wasn't just me. Chris and Will resented her as much as I did."

I saw the heavy-lidded weariness in her eyes, the old tautness around her mouth. Hoping she'd continue, I said, "What finally happened to them?"

She was playing with her fork, turning it over and over on the table. "One Friday night, my father got hit by a car right in front of McCloskey's, his favorite bar. He died a few days later, two weeks after my thirteenth birthday. It was a relief, to be honest. My mother went to work in the garment district, making blouses. She died from a cerebral hemorrhage six years later. By then, I was 19 and in my first year at Brooklyn College. Chris and Will were in high school."

"What about Uncle Will?" I asked. "He hasn't come to visit in so long."

My mother sighed again. "Well . . . you know, Grace . . . Uncle Will feels uncomfortable here. He really loved your father. Whenever he came, he felt like he was in the middle." She cleared her throat. "Now we just talk on the phone . . . sometimes." It was the only time she had mentioned my father since he left several weeks earlier.

She became quiet again. I got up and started clearing the dishes, hoping her mood would change. I hadn't meant to upset her. I wanted things to go on as they had been. I wanted to hear about the case studies she read for Group Dynamics and the community center hotline calls she answered. I wanted to ask about Uncle Chris and Uncle Will . . . and a hundred other things. I wanted to look up and see her sitting across the table from me, asking me questions, her face alive with interest. These quiet dinners—just the two of us—this was as good as I could imagine it being.

*   *   *

Erin and I, making our plans for college, spent hours paging through the books Miss Zrinsky had put aside for us. Although we talked about going away together, it seemed an unlikely possibility. With six kids in her family, Erin knew she'd have to attend a local college.

The fall of our senior year passed quickly. We were busy with school, going to football games and working on college applications. Erin, Molly and I joined the yearbook committee and were in charge of getting all the school clubs and special activities photographed. The three of us stayed late on Monday afternoons to work on the copy and captions. If a lot of the other kids were there, Miss Parker, the yearbook advisor, let us order pizza and hang out until the custodian made us leave at 6 o'clock.

Those few months were the most carefree of my life, being with my friends, working at the library with Miss Zrinsky, not having knots in my stomach at the thought of going home.

In a moment, on a random Wednesday morning, everything changed. When I arrived at school, I went to meet Erin at her locker, part of our daily ritual. She wasn't there. At noon, I tried calling her. No answer. After school and throughout the evening, I called again. Still nothing.

I couldn't imagine what had happened. Maybe her grandmother died. By Thursday morning, I couldn't concentrate. My nerves were rattled; the slightest noise startled me.

During economics, Andrea passed me a note. Did you see the article about Erin's father?

No. What??? I flipped my note onto her desk.

It's in today's Post. He was arrested.

A wave of nausea washed over me. After class, I ran out of school to buy the paper. It was a cold March day, even though the sun was shining, melting what was left of the snow. In my rush to get out, I had left my coat at school. I grabbed the paper from the corner news stand. There on page 7, the headline:

Queens Father of Six Charged in Domestic Dispute

Local police arrested insurance executive Harold Stevens for allegedly threatening his wife Carol with a kitchen knife in the early hours Wednesday morning. The police were summoned to the Stevens' residence by a 911 call from a neighbor. Stevens, 49, was arraigned in Queens criminal court and released.

I couldn't force myself back to class. Dazed, I went to my locker to get my coat, then walked home slowly, trying to figure out where Erin could be. When I got to my house, I didn't go in. Instead, I ran back to school. What if she came and I wasn't there?

I had missed all of English, lunch and most of gym. I waited at my locker for the bell to ring and went to physics. Then French. I gave up before math, my last class, and left again. I ran the three blocks to the library. Miss Zrinsky was sitting at the main desk. I almost shouted her name.

Startled, she looked up. Then she walked over to me.

"You already know, don't you?" I asked her.

She nodded. "I saw it in the paper."

"I can't find her, Miss Zrinsky." My throat felt parched. I tried to swallow. "She's not in school and nobody answers their phone."

She put her hand on my arm. "Maybe they went to a relative's. Where does her grandmother live?" she asked.

I stopped short, dumbfounded by my own ignorance. "I don't know. I don't know anything. I've only been in her house twice. In all these years." I started to cry. Every eye in the library turned toward me. On top of everything else, I was creating a scene.

"Grace, go wait for me in the back," Miss Zrinsky said softly. "I'll be there as soon as I can."

I went to the back office. I noticed a faint banana smell as I opened the door, then spotted the peel in the waste basket. I sat down at the table, a large, light-colored wood table, defaced with dozens of pen and pencil marks, as well as scratches of all sizes and the initials LMB etched in a corner. A few petals had dropped from the vase of violets on the table. I picked them up and tossed them in the garbage.

Here at this table, Erin and I had spent many hours sorting through books and updating catalogues. I closed my eyes. I wanted to imagine her standing in the doorway, but I couldn't get the picture in my head. I got up and walked to Miss Zrinsky's desk, taking some M & M's from the bowl she kept there for us. Then I walked to the window and looked out through the slats in the Venetian blinds. They smelled of dust. I heard the door open and Miss Zrinsky's voice. "How are you feeling?" she asked.

I shrugged. "I don't understand why she hasn't called me." My eyes searched Miss Zrinsky's face as if it held the answer.

"This must be a very hard time for Erin," she said. "I know she'll call you when she can."

I stood to leave. Miss Zrinsky said, "Grace, why don't you stay here awhile?"

"I can't sit still . . . I have to go home. Maybe she'll call."

She nodded and walked me to the door. "You will come back tomorrow?" she asked as I reached for the door knob.

"Yes," I said. "I'll come after school."

At home, I played the message on the answering machine. My mother—out with some of the people from her Group Dynamics class. She'd be home late. I could eat the left-over pot roast in the refrigerator.

I blinked back tears and picked up the phone to dial my father's number. Realizing Valerie would be there, I hung up. I walked into the family room and turned on the TV. I stared at the screen through the news and some stupid game show. Finally, I forced myself upstairs and pulled out my math homework. After I did most of it, I called Andrea. She didn't know anything new. I got into bed at 9 o'clock, two hours earlier than usual, and went to sleep.

The next morning, I heard my mother in the kitchen as I was getting ready to leave. She was sitting at the table in her quilted yellow robe, drinking from a large blue coffee mug, the newspaper spread out in front of her. She glanced over at me as I walked in.

"You ready to leave?" she asked.

"Mom, Erin's gone," I blurted out.

"What do you mean, gone?"

"She wasn't in school yesterday and she's not home. I haven't even heard from her!" I could hear the tremor in my voice.

"Well, don't worry, it's only been one day," she said, lowering her eyes back to the newspaper. "I'm sure she'll be back soon." Her voice faded as she turned the page and continued reading.

I felt like yanking the paper off the table. I grabbed my books from the counter and walked out, letting the door slam behind me.

On the way to school, I bought a paper and looked for news of Erin's family. Nothing. Then over the weekend, a second article appeared.

New Charges Pending For Queens Dad

Detectives investigating the domestic dispute in the Queens home of Harold Stevens, 49, reportedly uncovered several boxes containing pornographic photographs in the basement of the family's home.

Sources close to the District Attorney's office revealed that the photographs were of children, dating back an estimated ten years.

"Right now we are examining the evidence and attempting to identify the victims," said a police department spokesperson. "Neighbors and friends of the Stevens' children are being contacted."

Stevens was arrested last Wednesday for allegedly threatening his wife Carol, 47, with a kitchen knife. The six Stevens' children were at home at the time of the episode.

Pornographic photographs? Oh god, Erin.

I went to the corner and waited at the bus stop for the Q42 to Erin's. I got off at her corner and ran to her house. The shades on the front windows were drawn. I wanted her to be in there behind those shades. I rang the bell, watching for movement inside the house. Nothing. I walked around to the back. A two-toned tan station wagon was parked in the driveway. I went over to the garage and looked in the window. Another smaller, gray car was there, along with several bicycles.

Where were they?

I went back to the front and sank down on the porch steps. In the distance, everyone on the block looked like Erin. I imagined her in every passing car. One of them would stop. I would wait. Time passed slowly. Finally it was almost dark. I had been there for nearly two hours.

I rode the bus home in a daze. My own house was dark except for the light my mother always left on in the front hall. I knew she wouldn't be home before 10:30. Monday nights were her busiest, with two classes back-to-back.

I went up to my room and saw the message light flashing on the answering machine. I pressed play. My father's voice: "Hi, Grace. I was hoping to take you out for a hamburger tonight. Let's try for tomorrow night. Give me a call. Oh . . . and don't forget to call Gram. She expected to see you on Friday."

I closed the blinds and sat down on my bed. On top of everything else, I had forgotten to go to my grandmother's. I wanted to cry but the tears wouldn't come. The phone started to ring. I knew it wasn't Erin and didn't move to answer it. Still wearing my clothes, I got under the covers, shivering, until I fell asleep.

I was in the park watching Heather and Claudia Markham jump rope. I heard Erin's voice call my name. I turned around and saw her across the playground

on a swing. I started to run toward her, but I was stuck, knee-deep in a thick
mucky slime.

*   *   *

The days that followed seemed endless. I forced myself through familiar routines although nothing at all felt familiar. The kids at school kept asking me what I knew. Everyone assumed I had the inside scoop.

Two of Erin's neighbors, classmates of ours, told me they had been questioned by the police, but the police never contacted me. Even that would have been some sort of validation. There were moments I felt like I had imagined our entire friendship.

Each afternoon, I went to the library. Miss Zrinsky shook her head when I told her how my mother had brushed me off. "She goes to that community center and listens to all those people there . . . and everyone who calls in on the hot-line." She's fundamentally inadequate, I thought to myself.

"Grace, have you told your father about Erin?"

I shook my head. "I can't even imagine telling him. I mean . . . we don't talk . . . just about my school work and stuff. I don't think I want to. I mean . . . what if he just dismisses it?" My head hurt. I pressed my hand against my forehead.

*   *   *

Eight days after it all began, I got home from school to find Erin sitting on the steps outside my house, her red hair visible from halfway down the street. A surge of excitement rippled through my chest, then quickly dissolved into a gnawing dread. I walked up to her slowly as she looked up at me, her eyes brimming. I crouched in front of her and reached for her hand. For what felt like a long time, neither one of us spoke.

She lifted her forearm and covered her eyes. Then, squinting, she looked at me and said: "Please don't ask me anything."

"Okay," I whispered.

We went inside the house and into my bedroom. I put on my new Madonna album and started hanging up the clothes I had earlier dropped on the bed. I wanted to give Erin time to find her own space. After a few minutes, I sat down across from her.

"I missed you," I said. "I've been afraid for you."

Biting her lower lip, she struggled to stifle her tears. "I wanted to call," she said, "but it was . . . too hard."

"Where have you been?" I asked.

She pushed her hair from her face. "Three of us went to my uncle's in Brooklyn. My mother took the younger kids to my grandmother's in Trenton."

Trenton, New Jersey. I would remember that forever.

"There are too many of us so we had to split up."

"Are you at home now?" I asked.

She shook her head. "My mother doesn't want to go back there." She wiped her eyes with the back of her hand. I handed her a box of kleenex.

"What about school?" I asked, my anxiety spiking again.

She shrugged. Then in a thin, listless voice: "My mother said we have to sell the house. We can't afford it anyway. Not now."

I tried to breathe deeply to stave off the growing nausea. "Erin," I managed to whisper, struggling to keep my voice even. "How can this be happening?"

She didn't answer. She wiped her eyes again. "I'm so tired," she said. "I just need to lie down for a few minutes."

"Okay," I said. "I'll be in the kitchen."

I sat down at the table and took out my notebook. I had an essay comparing two Robert Frost poems due in English the next day. I couldn't concentrate. How could any of this end well? It didn't seem possible.

An hour later, I went back into my bedroom. Erin was lying on my bed, awake, staring at the wall.

"Erin," I said gently. "Stay here with me. It's only a few months 'til graduation."

She turned toward me. "How can I go back to school? Everyone knows. It's been in all the papers. It's hard enough without being a public spectacle." Then the after-thought: "Besides, my mother would never let me."

It felt pointless to argue with her. "What will you do?" I asked.

Her eyes were still fixed on the wall. "I don't know. My mother and my uncles are figuring out where each of us should live."

"Can you stay here tonight?" I asked.

She shook her head again. "I have to be back by 8 o'clock," she replied. "I better get going. Can you walk me to the subway?"

We started to walk, the very same route we had taken on countless unmemorable occasions. My throat felt tight, my mouth dry. I didn't even try to talk.

When we got to the subway, I held onto to her arm. "Erin," I said. "Please call me."

"I will," she said, then headed down the stairs. At the bottom, she turned and looked up at me. "It's why I never invited you over. So he couldn't get to you."

Then she turned and disappeared into the station.

November 3, 1986

Dear Grace,

I've been meaning to write—things have gotten so complicated. We've moved three times since I last saw you. It's hard to believe it's been seven months.

Before his trial, my father went to my grandmother's house and went nuts. I don't really know what happened but, whatever, my mother hasn't been the same since. She jumps at the slightest noise and locks herself in the bathroom for long periods of time. My youngest sister Caroline, who was there when he lost it, is still having nightmares and cries whenever my mother leaves the room.

Afterwards, my Uncle Jim (Brooklyn) decided we should move out of New York, even though they got a restraining order. Since then, we've been living with different relatives. Right now, my sister Kate and I are staying with cousins just outside of Kansas City. I'm in a teller-training program at a small bank where I've been working for about two months. Everything here is small. I feel like I'm living someone else's life. At this moment, going to college is out of the question. I haven't even gotten my high school diploma.

When I first wake up in the morning, I imagine myself in my bed in Queens, soon to be meeting you in front of our lockers. It's the best part of my day.

I know you must be away at school. I don't even know where you decided to go. I'm hoping your mother will forward this letter.

I miss you.

Love, Erin

March 11, 1987

Dear Grace,

I know you would've written if you had gotten my letter. I guess I can't count on your mother.

Good news—the manager at the bank has discovered that I can add and subtract and is promoting me to a higher-paying position. When Kate graduates from high school next year, she'll get a job and we'll try to find a small apartment. I don't know what I'd do if she wasn't here.

My mother and the other kids are living with two different sets of relatives. We aren't even in the same state. We'll try to meet at some mid-point in another month or two. I guess everyone's having a hard time.

I'm hoping you'll get my letters sooner or later. I'm sending telepathic messages to your mother.

Love, Erin

June 12, 1987

Dear Grace,

I am really disgusted with your mother.

Things are moving along here in their own way. My new job at the bank is fairly interesting so the time passes more quickly. Also, I am actually making a friend, a girl (Ruth) who works at the real estate agency a few doors from the bank. We struck up a conversation one day at the coffee shop and, since then, have met for lunch twice. She is looking for someone to share an apartment with, but I told her I can't leave Kate.

My Uncle Jim has arranged for me to do independent study to make up the work I missed at the end of our senior year. I might actually become a high school graduate in this decade. Hard to imagine it comes to this . . . after three years in the National Honor Society.

Love, Erin

December 14, 1987

Dear Grace,

Terrible news. We've just been told that my mother had a breakdown and is in a county hospital outside of Omaha. She's been living in Omaha with my sister Caroline and brother Timmy. I guess you may not remember him—he's the youngest of the six of us.

I don't even know what it means to have a "breakdown." I can only picture an abandoned car on the shoulder of some highway with steam pouring out from under the hood.

My uncles have sold our house in Queens and some of that money will pay for my mother's medical care. She hasn't had any health insurance since my father became a convicted felon.

The money from the house was supposed to buy a place where we could all live together again. Now that's not going to happen. I'm wondering if this nightmare is ever going to end.

I hate my father.

I need you to write.

Love, Erin

January 21, 1988

Dear Grace,

Last night I realized I could mail the letters to Miss Zrinsky which I can't believe I didn't think of sooner.

More changes. I am moving from Kansas next week. The family has decided (since I'm the oldest) that I should move to Omaha to be with Caroline and Timmy. Nobody knows when my mother will be better.

Kate will be staying here in Kansas to finish high school. There's not enough room for her at my great aunt's house in Omaha anyway.

I can't believe we're being separated. I tell myself things can't get any worse, but they do. They get worse.

I miss you.

Love, Erin

April 2, 1988

Dear Erin,

Where should I begin? Miss Zrinsky sent me your letter. Then I came home for spring break and found your earlier letters in a drawer in the dining room breakfront. They were mixed together with a bunch of bills.

I grabbed the whole stack, walked into the family room where my mother was watching TV and dropped them on her lap.

She said—Oh, I was saving these for you.

I said—for a year-and-a-half? She eventually admitted to having forgotten about them. I felt like strangling her.

I'm so sorry you had to leave Kate. I wish I could do something to help you.

Please write as soon as you can. I think of you constantly.

Love, Grace

P.S. My address:

Syracuse University

Flint 4A

Mt. Olympus Drive

Syracuse, NY 13210

April 28, 1988

Dear Erin,

I'm upset that I haven't heard from you. I can see how you must have felt not hearing from me for over a year.

In another month, I'll be finishing my second year at Syracuse. It's been good for me here. I've made some close friends—my roommate (Lila) and two other girls—one lives down the hall (Pam) and the other was in my Geology lab (Eve). The four of us have signed up for a suite together next year. I've told them all about you—even showed them your senior class picture.

I'm happy to be away from home. I hate going back even for short vacations. My mother lives alone in our house on Wentworth Street. Things between us were good in the beginning when my father first left. But she lets me down in major ways. She's like a stranger. She talks and talks about her work at the community center and the families there. She tells me their names and which family member died. I want to say to her—do you **even know** what I'm majoring in? Do you know how Vanessa is?

Now she's brought out pictures of George—ones I've never seen before. She put them in one of those big rectangular-framed collages and hung it on a wall in her bedroom. She has my graduation picture on her dresser. None of Vanessa.

Sometimes I stay at my father's. I give him advance notice so what's-her-name Valerie won't be there. He knows I won't stay with him if she's there. It isn't that I care about him being with her—I just don't think I should have to deal with her.

Vanessa has her own apartment in Jackson Heights—a large studio with a sleeping alcove—perfect for one person and only a 30 minute subway ride to her job in Manhattan. She just changed jobs recently and is working at an ad agency. When I'm home, we go shopping or to a movie. Last month she took me to a club, The Tunnel, with dancing and live music. It was pretty wild—lots of people were smoking dope and looked totally spaced-out. Once in a while, we have dinner out with my father or go to my grandmother's for one of her big feasts.

I can't believe it has been two years since I've seen you.

There isn't anything I wouldn't give . . .

Love, Grace

August 12, 1988

Dear Erin,

I've been frantically trying to find you. I thought of calling your grandmother in Trenton until I realized I don't even know her last name.

I made myself nuts for a while—then Miss Zrinsky helped me do a search of the archives at the Bureau of Public Records. We estimated your mother's birth date from the newspaper article and found her maiden name, Wylie. I called every Wylie in the Brooklyn phone directory until I found your uncle. My name seemed to ring a remote bell in his memory. He told me to send my letter to him.

I spoke to my Dad—he said you are welcome to stay with him if you come back. He has three bedrooms—you would have plenty of privacy. Miss Zrinsky will help you look for financial aid so you could go to Queens College. I will stay with you on all my vacations—even if Valerie is there. When I graduate, we can get our own place.

What can I say to convince you?

Love, Grace

September 16, 1989

Dear Grace,

You probably hate me. I should've written to you a year ago. I didn't want to be a failure in your eyes, but I guess I'm a coward.

Please thank your father for his very generous offer. I don't want him (or you) to think I didn't appreciate it.

I don't even know where to begin. After I got to Omaha, I really hit bottom. Caroline (9 yrs old) cried and sucked her thumb most of the day. Timmy threw temper tantrums and wet the bed. My Great Aunt Rebecca made it quite clear that we had used up her good will. Not that I blame her. Who would want to have three strangers move into their house?

I tried to keep the kids quiet and out of her way. It was exhausting—and time consuming. I couldn't get a full-time job. I'm embarrassed to say I didn't even finish the work for my diploma.

When Caroline and Timmy were in school, I worked as a cashier in the supermarket to cover the mid-day lunch breaks of the regulars. Then I'd pick up the kids from school and keep them outside for as long as possible. My whole life was about other people's needs and demands. I felt like I was disappearing. Everything that was important to me seemed irrelevant. There were days I could barely speak.

When your letter came, I sank further. Of course, I desperately wanted to get out of here, but I couldn't leave the kids. I didn't have the energy to make you understand that there was no one here to take care of them. I know you believed I had a choice, but I really didn't.

My mother was discharged from Sagamore County Hospital about two weeks after I got here. I felt hugely relieved and actually thought I'd be able to go back to Kansas City. Well, that turned out to be pie in the fucking sky.

My mother stayed in her room most of the time and had an eerie zombie-like blank look on her face. She barely responded to any of us which upset Caroline and Timmy even more than they already were. By the end of the first week, my Uncle Jim flew out here and took her back to Trenton to my grandmother's.

Then I met Calvin Springer, this guy who came into the supermarket to buy his lunch at the deli counter. He's one of the mechanics at the gas station around the corner from the market. We started to talk and joke around. One night I took the kids to the park and he was there playing softball. Afterwards he walked us home.

I began sneaking out to see him after the kids were asleep. He was the only person in my life who didn't make things harder. I thought about him all the time.

A couple of months later, I discovered I was pregnant. I honest-to-god wanted to die. There wasn't even anyone I could tell. I was afraid Aunt Rebecca's would throw us out. I didn't know what to do. The worst was early in the morning—just as I was waking up and remembering the mess I'd made.

Finally I broke down and told Calvin. We were married a month later. We took Caroline and Timmy and moved into an apartment over the garage of his parents' house. I was so anxious to get out of Aunt Rebecca's, I didn't really stop to figure out how this arrangement would work. Not very well is the answer.

Calvin's father complained about the noise. The kids trampled some of his flowers and left their toys in the driveway. Calvin complained about the lack of privacy. Only his mother didn't complain. She tried to help me in every possible way. She was the one who encouraged me to speak to my mother.

So I did. I called her and told her we needed to talk. She must've known something big was coming because right away she started telling me how much she appreciated what I was doing, how she needed more time, how I should just hang on awhile longer.

I said, "No. You can't do this anymore. You have children who need you. We're falling apart without you. I can't take your place. You need to get on a plane and come back here. Today."

Then I started to cry. I cried for a long time—right into the phone so she'd hear everything. When I was done, I heard her crying on her end. Then, in a small voice, she said, "Okay."

The next week she came back and moved into Aunt Rebecca's. Everyday I took the kids there to see her. A few weeks later, they went to live with her. She's finding ways to cope. She sees a psychiatrist and takes pills for depression. She's also in family therapy with Caroline and Timmy.

Meanwhile, the baby is due next month. I can assure you—it shocks me as much as it must be shocking you.

Everything that's happened has taken me further away from what I think of as my real life. I think I understand now that I'm not going to get back there.

I hope you aren't angry or disappointed in me. In my other life, I thought things were either black or white, right or wrong. Now everything feels mostly gray. Every imaginable shade of gray.

I miss you.

Love, Erin

Vanessa

Ten years later, my father and I sat next to each other in a New York criminal courtroom, directly behind Vanessa. She was at the defense table with her lawyer, whose name (Douglas Newton) I learned earlier that morning. Since they had their backs to us, I didn't get a good look at her face on that first day, but I could see her hands folded on the table in front of her, the sleeves of her black suit contrasting with her pale skin. Her blond hair, somewhat darker now, was pulled back into a clip at her neck. She sat very still, not moving except to lean, whispering, toward her lawyer. I imagined her face, shrouded with fear and apprehension, her eyes bleary and baffled. But when she looked directly at us the following day, it wasn't fear I saw but anger, in her narrowed eyes and tight pinched lips, the same look she used to flash at my mother during a fight. I shifted in my seat, suppressing a sudden urge to leave.

But I wasn't there for Vanessa; I was there so my father wouldn't be alone. I felt sorry for him for the way he suffered over her. I guess some part of me still wanted his approval. And . . . I won't deny wanting to see for myself what this whole ugly mess was about. So I took a two-week vacation from my job as a recruiter for American Express and met my father in front of the court building in lower Manhattan.

I held my breath when I saw the nine men and five women file into the jury box. Beside me, my father slowly shook his head. Four of the men looked to be under forty, not much older than Vanessa who had turned thirty-five last month. I watched them look at her, every one of them smiling. Already she had an edge.

Next to me, my father had fixated on his key chain, trying to straighten a single bent link between his thumb and index finger. He glanced over at the jury only briefly, then took a deep breath and looked away. You don't deserve this, I wanted to say.

The prosecutor, a man by the name of Fred Kelly, called his first witness, Simone Agnelli, a woman of striking beauty—tall, shoulder-length black hair, dark eyes, deep red lipstick. I knew Vanessa wouldn't like this woman who could turn as many heads as Vanessa herself.

"Are you acquainted with the defendant, Vanessa Strickland?" Kelly asked, motioning toward Vanessa. He looked about 35 years old, with a boyish face and large, black-framed glasses.

"Yes, I am."

"How do you know her?" he continued.

She looked directly at Vanessa with an expression conveying unadulterated disgust. "We worked at the same company."

"Please describe to the court your dealings with Miss Strickland," Kelly said, adjusting his glasses. When he turned to face us, I could see what looked like a safety pin holding the frame together.

"Several months ago, she began coming to my office requesting appointments to see Mr. Wheatley. She . . ."

"Excuse me for interrupting you, Miss Agnelli, but who is Mr. Wheatley?" Kelly asked. He walked back to his table and grabbed a folder.

"He's my boss," she answered.

"What is Mr. Wheatley's position in the company?" asked Kelly, paging through his papers.

She sat back in her chair. "Senior vice president for international accounts."

"Okay. You were saying that the defendant wanted to see Mr. Wheatley?" Kelly asked, underscoring the point.

"Yes."

"Did she say why she wanted to see him?"

"No."

"Did you give her the appointments?"

"Yes."

"Do you know what transpired during these meetings?" Kelly asked.

"No."

"Miss Agnelli, what else can you tell us about your direct dealings with Vanessa Strickland?"

Kelly turned his back to her and walked toward the jury. A short man with a slight build, he was wearing a brown suit with out-dated cuffed pants. From across the room, I could see his tan socks peeking out over the top of his shoes.

"Well, one evening . . . I had already left work, but I went back to my office to get something." Simone was looking at Fred Kelly, who stood in front of the jury box. "I found her in Mr. Wheatley's office, looking through his rolodex."

My father and I exchanged nervous glances. I wondered what he was thinking. Hearing all this stuff was not going to be easy for him.

"What happened then?" Kelly pressed.

"I asked her what she was doing. I guess I startled her because she looked embarrassed."

Embarrassed? Maybe Simone Agnelli thought Vanessa should be embarrassed, but the Vanessa I knew would think nothing of going into someone else's office and looking through their things.

"Objection, your honor." Vanessa's lawyer was on his feet. "The witness has no way of knowing what Miss Strickland was feeling."

"Sustained. The jury will disregard the witness' last remark," said the judge. Judge Wilma Sudderfield looked nothing like what I'd imagined when I'd first seen her name outside the courtroom. I was expecting an older woman with sensible oxford shoes and thick opaque eye glasses, but when a tall beautiful woman emerged from the judge's chambers, I actually looked at her twice. It would unnerve Vanessa, I knew, to have to compete for attention with both the judge and Simone Agnelli.

"Did you report this incident to Mr. Wheatley?" Kelly asked.

"Yes," Miss Agnelli responded. "I told him the next morning. He said I should keep his office locked whenever he's out."

"Let's move to February 3, 1998. Did you have any dealings with Miss Strickland on that evening?" asked Kelly.

"Yes. I was working late . . . Mr. Wheatley was out of the office. His private line kept ringing. Every two or three minutes, it rang again—15, 20 rings at a time. It was incessant," she said.

"Objection."

"Sustained," the judge responded, looking over at Simone Agnelli. "Miss Agnelli, please confine your answers to the facts."

Kelly resumed. "Did you answer Mr. Wheatley's private line?"

"I finally did, yes. I don't usually answer that phone but it seemed . . ." She stopped herself and looked at Vanessa's lawyer.

"What happened when you answered it?" Kelly asked.

"The caller hung up. Then nothing happened for about 30 minutes. After that, it started ringing again."

"Did you answer it?" asked Kelly.

"Yes."

"Please tell the court what happened," Kelly said.

Simone Agnelli looked directly at Vanessa. "It was the defendant. She was screaming into the phone. She said: 'Put him on the fucking phone!'"

I could hear Vanessa saying it. I leaned over to watch her reaction but could only see the back of her head. I looked at the jury. They were all watching her.

"What did you say to her?" Kelly continued.

"Nothing. I hung up."

"Did anything else happen?" asked Kelly.

"Yes. Then she called on my line, I mean—you know, the regular office line. She was shrieking: 'Where is he? You better tell me where he is!'"

"What, if anything, did you say to her?" asked Kelly.

She shifted in the chair and cleared her throat. "I told her he was out of the office for the day. She said she didn't believe me. She was still screaming. She said she was coming down to my office."

"What happened next?" Kelly continued.

"I called security," she said. "A few minutes later, I heard her voice in the corridor arguing with the security guard."

"Thank you, Miss Agnelli," Kelly said. "I have no more questions at this time."

Douglas Newton, a tall, handsome man with wire-framed glasses, stood up and walked toward the jury, smiling. He wore a stylish blue pin-striped suit.

"Miss Agnelli," he began. "You stated that Miss Strickland had requested appointments to see Mr. Wheatley. Isn't it a fact that she served on a committee within his purview?"

"Yes."

"Isn't it possible that she wanted to discuss with Mr. Wheatley issues arising from the committee meetings?" he asked.

"I don't know what they discussed."

"I direct your attention to the evening of February 3 when you answered Mr. Wheatley's private phone," Newton continued. "Did Miss Strickland identify herself on the telephone?"

"I don't think so."

"Then how do you know it was she?" he asked.

"I know her voice."

"Miss Agnelli, would you say that Vanessa Strickland is a friend of yours, or perhaps even a close acquaintance?" he asked.

"No."

"How many conversations would you say you've had with her?"

"I'm not sure. Maybe six or eight."

"So after six or eight conversations, you state with certainty that the caller was Vanessa Strickland?" Newton asked, feigning disbelief.

"Yes. It was definitely her."

*   *   *

The next day, I had to stop by my office to drop off some reports, so I didn't get to the courtroom until mid-morning. I saw my father in the second row, his curly brown hair now mixed with gray, and slipped into the seat next to him. He held a small spiral note pad. I leaned over him and read the two words he had written—Agnelli, Davis.

A representative from the telephone company, a squat, heavy-set man in a light gray suit was on the witness stand. I couldn't take my eyes off his neck, so fat it spilled over the top of his shirt collar. His face was puffy and uncomfortably red—like he was about to explode. I put my hand up to my own neck.

"Mr. Davis, what is your position at NYNEX?" asked Kelly.

"I am the supervisor of the Annoyance Call Unit."

"What is the purpose and function of this Annoyance Call Unit?" Kelly asked.

"When customers file complaints with us that they are receiving harassing or obscene phone calls, we put a trap on their phone lines in order to identify the caller," Mr. Davis explained.

"Please describe the circumstances resulting in your identification of Vanessa Strickland as an annoyance caller," Kelly said.

So that's what she is . . . an annoyance caller, I thought to myself. I hadn't realized there was an official name for it.

Mr. Davis flipped open a manila folder and began reading from a computer print-out. "On January 7, 1998, Michael Wheatley filed a complaint that he was receiving harassing phone calls on two separate lines at his residence, one listed in his own name and the second in the name of his daughter, Samantha Wheatley. He also reported receiving annoyance calls on his office telephone at the Ameri-Zone Corporation."

"Did your office put traps on all three lines?" asked Kelly.

"Actually, we put traps on four lines, two at his residence and two in his office," Mr. Davis responded.

"Will you summarize for us what the traps revealed?" Kelly asked.

Mr. Davis continued reading from his notes. "One hundred forty-seven calls were made from the telephone at Vanessa Strickland's residence to the telephone listed in the name of Michael Wheatley at his residence. Eighteen calls were made from the telephone at Vanessa Strickland's residence to the telephone listed in the name of Samantha Wheatley," said Mr. Davis.

I glanced at my father. He was looking down at his hands, fidgeting with the spiral wire from his little notebook. He didn't look at me. Had he known this was coming? Gently, I touched his arm.

"With respect to the calls to Samantha Wheatley's phone—was there a pattern in the timing?" Kelly asked.

"Yes," said Mr. Davis. "With the exception of two calls, they were all made between the hours of 3:00 and 5:00 a.m.," said Mr. Davis.

"In the middle of the night?" Kelly queried.

"Yes."

My father started to cough, his body tensing next to me. I stared at Vanessa. This crosses the line, I thought to myself. Even for you.

"Please continue with your report, Mr. Davis," Kelly said.

"Twenty-three calls were made from the telephone at Vanessa Strickland's residence to the private line in Michael Wheatley's office. And four hundred forty-two calls were made from the telephone in Vanessa Strickland's office to Michael Wheatley's private line in his office," said Mr. Davis.

Kelly walked across the room and stood in front of the table where Vanessa was sitting. "Mr. Davis, what is the total count of the calls made from the defendant's telephones to the various telephones in Michael Wheatley's home and office?"

"Six hundred forty-four calls."

I took a deep breath. God, Vanessa. I looked at my father. He was shaking his head; his eyes were closed. I remembered going to see her at Hartwick some 13 years earlier, reading the letter from Timothy Hamer's lawyer. Then I had been shocked by 120 phone calls. I glanced over at her. Hands folded, she sat unmoving though she had begun chewing on her lower lip. How could she stand this? What if she goes to jail? It was too shocking to imagine.

"Six hundred and forty-four calls?" Kelly repeated, verbally underscoring each word.

"Objection," said Vanessa's lawyer. "The witness has already stated the number of phone calls."

"Sustained."

"I have no further questions of this witness," said Kelly.

Douglas Newton rose quickly, took off his glasses and walked briskly toward the witness.

"Mr. Davis, do you have any proof that it was actually Vanessa Strickland who made these calls and not someone using her phone?" he asked.

"No."

"Thank you. That will be all," said Newton, as he walked back to his chair and sat down next to Vanessa.

Judge Sudderfield banged her gavel and announced a lunch break. My father and I remained seated while the other spectators got up to leave. We watched Vanessa retreat, her back to us, as she and her lawyer left the courtroom through a door marked **Authorized Personnel.** She didn't once turn to look at us.

Each day my father seemed puzzled anew by her lack of acknowledgment. He, of course, was the one she had called when two New York City detectives knocked on her door and arrested her. He made the 45-minute drive that Sunday evening to the first precinct in lower Manhattan to pick her up and take her back to his apartment. He found Dr. Helene Caldwell, the psychiatrist she was now seeing, as well as Douglas Newton, whose bills he was paying. I hated her for ignoring him. I tugged gently on his sleeve.

"Let's get some lunch," I said softly. "You know she's embarrassed," I said. "Don't take it personally."

He turned toward me, frowning. "Six-hundred and forty-four calls," he said. "I don't understand . . ."

"I know," I said. "I don't either. She just doesn't let go."

*　　*　　*

In the afternoon session, Kelly called Samantha Wheatley as his next witness. I didn't know then how old she was, but she looked like a young child, fresh-faced and wholesome. Her light brown hair was drawn back into a pony tail which hung just past her shoulders onto her white blouse and green plaid vest. She wore a matching plaid pleated skirt. A parochial school uniform, wholly out of place in a witness chair.

After being sworn in, she sat down and looked cautiously over to Fred Kelly, her green eyes wide, nervous. It was hard to imagine Vanessa winning this match-up.

"Samantha, how old are you?" Kelly began.

"I'm thirteen." She sat up straight and smiled, as though proud of her age.

"Samantha, do you know Vanessa Strickland?" asked Kelly.

"Yes. Uh . . . I mean no. I don't know her but I know who she is."

"Please explain that to us," Kelly continued.

"She's the person who tried to get my father to leave us."

"Objection!" boomed Douglas Newton.

"Sustained," said the judge, who looked disapprovingly at Kelly. "The jury will disregard the witness' last statement."

"Samantha, have you ever spoken to a woman you believe to be Vanessa Strickland?" asked Kelly.

"Yes."

"Please tell the court about your first conversation with her," Kelly said.

"Well . . . um . . . one night my telephone woke me up. I looked at the clock and it was 4:28. There was a woman on the other end. She told me to get my father."

"Did you get your father?" Kelly asked.

"Well . . . no. I didn't know what to do. She said she was a . . . um . . . friend of his. I told her I couldn't get him, that it was the middle of the night. She kept saying it was very important. I told her to call him on his phone. She got very angry . . . uh . . . she started yelling at me. 'Samantha, you better get him!' I asked her how she knew my name. She said she knew a lot about me. It scared me. I hung up on her."

"When did this happen?" Kelly asked.

"I'm not sure, exactly. Um . . . maybe six months ago," said Samantha.

"Did you get other calls from this same woman?" asked Kelly.

"Yes," said Samantha. "Sometimes she hung up when I answered. After she woke me up. It was always in the middle of the night. A few times she played . . . uh . . . you know . . . tape recordings."

"Tell us about the tape recordings," Kelly said.

"Most of them were pretty fuzzy," Samantha said.

"Were any of them clear?" Kelly's voice became softer.

With the heel of her hand, Samantha began pressing down on the pleats in her skirt. "Yes," she said, finally looking up.

"Please tell us what you heard on the recordings," Kelly urged.

Samantha looked at Kelly. "Um . . ." She looked down again, into her lap. "They were all . . . my father's voice was on all of them." She was biting her lip, playing with her pleats. For a few seconds, I thought she might start crying. Every eye in the courtroom was on her.

"What was your father saying?" Kelly asked.

She started to cough and cupped her hands over her mouth. Kelly walked back to his table and poured a glass of water. "Take your time, Samantha," he said, handing her the glass. The court room was silent as Samantha drank the water.

Judge Sudderfield leaned toward Samantha. "Do you need more time?"

Samantha shook her head.

"Let's continue," the judge said to Fred Kelly.

"Samantha, can you tell us what your father said on the tapes?" Kelly asked.

She sat very still. Then she turned to the judge and said, "Do I have to talk about this?"

"Yes, Samantha, you do. Didn't Mr. Kelly explain all of this to you?" Judge Sudderfield's voice had softened.

Samantha nodded. "I forgot the question."

The judge motioned to the court stenographer, who reached for the tape behind her machine and read aloud: "Samantha, can you tell us what your father said on the tapes?"

Samantha continued to stare at her pleats. "Things like . . . um . . . I can't wait to see you. I can't stop thinking about you." She was almost whispering.

I felt a sudden surge of anger and held my breath as I swung around in my seat toward Vanessa. I wanted to yell at her then and there—for calling this young girl in the middle of the night. Eighteen times. A thirteen year old! It was unimaginable.

I looked over at my father. He was staring at the back of Vanessa's head. Then he closed his eyes.

"Samantha, did you have any other dealings with the defendant, Miss Strickland, besides the phone calls?" Kelly asked.

"Yes," she said. "One day . . . um . . . I was leaving school . . . she came up to me."

"Where do you go to school?" asked Kelly.

"Xavier Junior High School."

"Please go on, Samantha," Kelly said. "Tell the jury what Miss Strickland said to you."

Samantha looked at Vanessa, then quickly back at Kelly. "She handed me an envelope and told me to give it to my father."

"Did you know who she was?" Kelly asked.

"No, not then. I found out later."

"Did you open the envelope?" Kelly asked.

"Yes," said Samantha. "It was a note. It said . . . um . . . 'you aren't as smart as you think you are. I can get to Samantha or Margot any time I feel like it.'"

"Who is Margot?" Kelly asked.

"My ten-year-old sister."

"Do you see the person who handed you this envelope in the courtroom today?" Kelly asked.

Samantha sat forward in the chair and pointed directly at Vanessa. "It's her," she said, with sudden forcefulness. She continued to stare at Vanessa, her eyes challenging.

My father stood up and walked out briskly, his footsteps echoing in the high-ceilinged room. I turned around and watched him push his way through the swinging doors. Two women stared at me from across the courtroom. My face flushed. They seemed to know who I was. I'm not responsible for her, I wanted to say. I looked away. Maybe she should go to jail, I thought. What else is going to stop her?

Douglas Newton walked over to Samantha. "Samantha, I just have a few questions," he began.

She looked up at him, then past him to where Vanessa sat.

"You testified that you spoke to Miss Strickland several times. Is that correct?" he asked.

"Yes."

"Did Miss Strickland ever identify herself on the phone? Did she tell you her name?" Newton asked.

"No."

"Then how do you know who you were talking to?" Newton asked.

Bewildered, Samantha looked over at Fred Kelly.

"Just answer the question, please," said Newton.

"I'm not sure. I think . . . uh . . . my mother told me. After I found out . . . uh . . . about her and my father," said Samantha.

"Your mother told you it was Miss Strickland on the phone?" Newton said, underscoring every word.

"Well . . . yes. I mean . . . I think so."

"Was your mother there when you received these phone calls?"

"No," said Samantha.

"So how would your mother know who you were on the phone with?" asked Newton.

"Objection. Calls for a conclusion from the witness," Fred Kelly interjected.

"Sustained."

"Samantha, you don't really know who was on the phone with you, do you?" asked Newton.

"No," she said, barely above a whisper.

*   *   *

The next morning, I sat across from my father in a diner a block from the courthouse. The dark circles under his eyes made him look ten years older. My mind flashed back to a much younger face—vibrant and handsome—my father's face as he walked with the woman I now know as Valerie Costas at the Third Avenue Street Fair.

"Dad, you know . . . it feels like . . . I mean . . . a lot of things are . . . well, maybe this isn't the best time. But I've been thinking about Vanessa . . . all of us, really . . . and there are some things I've been wanting to ask you. For a long time."

He looked at me as he stirred his coffee. "Okay, go ahead."

"How come you waited so long to leave? I mean . . ." I hesitated.

"Go on, Grace. Just say what's on your mind," he said, raising the cup to his mouth.

"I've always wondered what would've happened if that awful scene between Vanessa and Mom had never taken place. I mean . . . would you have just stayed?"

He sat back and looked at me, his eyebrows raised. "Grace, where is this coming from?"

"I don't know. I mean . . . it's something I've wondered about," I said. "It seemed like everything blew up so suddenly."

He didn't answer immediately. "I probably would have stayed longer," he said finally. He was looking down, brushing something off his pants. "I thought it was my responsibility to take care of your mother . . . and you and Vanessa. I was very worried about Vanessa, even early on. Her behavior was so . . . erratic. I was afraid of what would happen if the family broke up."

I watched him pick up his knife and spread blueberry jam, his favorite, on his toast. I pressed my back into the cushioned fabric of the booth and watched him eat. It was a familiar sight. Through the years, we had met every few weeks for dinner, sometimes lunch, at one diner or another, trading tid-bits of news. He'd tell me about a bridge he was working on in Iowa, or how he'd beaten Peter Desmond in tennis. He'd ask me about my job . . . or if I'd seen Vanessa.

"Did you know she trashed the doll house you gave me?" I leaned forward and studied his face. His hair was thinning in the front. I wondered why I hadn't noticed it before.

He dropped his toast on the plate. "Of course. I still think about that sometimes. I knew Vanessa got most of the attention. I wanted to make it up to you. I gave you the biggest gift I could find," he said.

I felt sudden tears behind my eyelids. I looked down at my English muffin, cold on the plate. "You knew?" I was shaking my head. "All these years, I told myself you didn't know. I wanted to believe you didn't know."

He looked at me, puzzled. "Who else could it have been?" He missed the point entirely.

"But if you knew . . . why didn't you **say something** to her? You just let her get away with it."

He sat back and looked at me, apparently surprised by my sudden anger. "I was afraid of what would happen if I punished her. She was like . . . I don't know . . . volatile. So unpredictable."

"But it was at **my** expense." I looked back down at my English muffin. There was nowhere to go with this. I was afraid to go on. He was all I had.

"I see you're upset. It was a long time ago, Grace."

"It . . . was my childhood. I was way down in your priorities. You chose to help Vanessa . . . every single time . . . it was Vanessa. You never held her accountable for anything."

"That's why I gave you the doll house—not Vanessa. Because I wanted to make it up to you."

"I needed more than a dollhouse. I needed ground rules we all had to live by. I needed a level playing field."

He shook his head slowly, no longer looking at me. I knew I should let it go, but I couldn't. It had taken me all these years to stand up for myself.

"I needed the protection you gave to Vanessa. I needed you to make sure that I had rights too."

He was staring at his coffee cup.

"You once said that I never accepted Valerie." I was now flinging the words at him. "You know why? Because I was always at the back of the line. First you abandoned me for Vanessa. Then you abandoned me for Valerie. It was never my turn."

I stopped talking. I listened to the clanging plates as the waitress cleared the tables around us. I was beginning to feel guilty for saying all this now, when he had so many other things to deal with.

"Grace, I am an imperfect man," he said, looking directly at me. "I did the wrong things . . . too many times. You deserved better." His voice was low, almost hoarse.

I didn't say anything. I would forgive my father, but not today. The man who sat across the table from me was not the man I had wanted him to be.

He pulled some money out of his wallet and laid it on the table. "You want to go back?" he asked.

I took my time responding. "I think I'll meet you in the morning," I said. "I need a break from this."

* * *

The next morning I entered the courtroom late. My father had taken a seat behind Fred Kelly's table and from that angle, we could see Vanessa's profile, her perfect features. She'd been given every advantage, or so it seemed. Why had it come to this? I slipped in next to my father and gave him a weak smile. It was all I could manage.

Samantha's mother, Christina Wheatley, sat in the witness chair. A slightly overweight, pleasant-looking woman in her mid-forties, she looked old-fashioned next to Vanessa. She wore a navy suit with a simple gold pin on the jacket. At her neckline, I could see a small gold cross.

She kept shifting in her seat, looking pained and uncomfortable, crossing and uncrossing her legs at regular intervals. When she spoke, she had noticeable trouble swallowing. She fidgeted with her purse and, from time to time played with her hair, twirling a few strands around her index finger.

Kelly was standing in front of her. "Mrs. Wheatley, please describe in your own words your dealings with Vanessa Strickland over the past several months."

Holding a handkerchief she had pulled from her purse, she began, speaking softly, with visible discomfort. "It started with the phone calls. At first mostly hang-ups. Dozens of phone calls."

"Mrs. Wheatley, were you aware that your husband was having a romantic relationship with Miss Strickland?" Kelly asked.

"Not at first. Not when the calls first started, but sometime after that." She seemed to be trying to keep her eyes on Kelly but they kept dropping down to her hands which clutched the purse in her lap.

"How, exactly, did you learn about their relationship?" he asked.

She shifted in her chair. "I . . . um . . . well, one afternoon, I went home and found a phone message. It was her voice on our answering machine." She stopped speaking, her gaze now burrowed into her lap.

"Mrs. Wheatley," Kelly said softly. "Please tell us about the message."

Christina looked up at him. "The message . . . it was a woman's voice . . . she said, 'I thought you should know what a great lover Michael is. He says that sex with me is the best he's ever had.' Then she laughed."

Christina Wheatley pressed her knuckles against her lips, her eyes still fixed on the purse in her lap.

The room was absolutely still. "Tell us what happened next," Kelly urged.

"I played the tape for Michael that night," she said.

"What did he say?" asked Kelly.

"Well, at first, he pretended not to know anything about it. But that was so ridiculous . . ." She stopped and looked briefly at the jury, sighing loudly. "The next morning he finally admitted that he'd had an affair with her. He told me she threatened him when he tried to end it, that she was blackmailing him."

"Objection," said Newton.

"Sustained." The judge looked down at Christina Wheatley, then over at Vanessa. I wondered what she was thinking.

Kelly continued. "Mrs. Wheatley, let's get back to your direct dealings with the defendant. What happened after that first message?"

"The phone calls continued," she said. "Sometimes she hung up. Sometimes she said things." Christina Wheatley's eyes were now on Fred Kelly.

"How did you respond to these calls?" asked Kelly.

"Uh . . . well, most of the time I hung up. One time, when she asked to speak to Michael, I told her he wasn't available. She said, 'He's a lot more available than you think.'"

I shook my head. You're merciless, Vanessa, I thought to myself.

"Please continue," said Kelly.

"Uh . . . she left a number of messages on the answering machine. She talked about things they had done . . . um . . . sexual things." Mrs. Wheatley's face suddenly flushed; she looked away from Kelly. I watched her hands in constant motion, fidgeting with her cross, the clasp on her purse. It was hard not to feel sorry for her.

"Please go on," Kelly said.

Christina took a deep breath. "She talked . . . uh . . . about gifts he gave her . . . and restaurants they went to. And . . . oh . . . a weekend trip they took." She shifted in her chair and coughed. "She kept talking about . . . um . . . the sex. And pictures they took of each other."

Kelly introduced the tape recordings into evidence, tapes of Vanessa's voice saying the very things Christina Wheatley described. Every juror was looking at Vanessa. The evidence seemed insurmountable.

"Was that the end of the calls?" asked Kelly.

"No, no. Not the end. Sometime after that, she began leaving recordings of his voice . . . um . . . on our answering machine."

"Your Honor, the State would now like to play these tapes for the jury," Kelly said.

"Mr. Newton?" the judge said.

"No objection," Douglas Newton responded.

In succession, three short tapes were played for the jury. The same male voice could be heard on each tape.

"Hey sexy. I love those delicious short skirts. Wear the black one tomorrow, sweetheart."

*   *   *

"I dreamt about you last night. You walked into my office in your purple bra and panties."

*   *   *

"I can't stop thinking about you. You drive me crazy. I need to see you."

I watched the jurors' faces as they listened to the recordings. Some looked at Vanessa, some at Christina Wheatley. What were they thinking? Were they shocked? Vanessa had been doing this sort of thing since we were kids—ruining things for people. She couldn't just have an affair and be done with it. She had to drag his whole family through it. Expose them to every excruciatingly sordid detail. I looked over at my father. He sat motionless.

Kelly asked Christina Wheatley to confirm her husband's voice. Her eyes were closed, her humiliation palpable.

The judge's voice broke through the silence. "Court will be in recess for thirty minutes."

*   *   *

Christina Wheatley again took the stand after the break and Fred Kelly continued questioning her.

"Did you ever have a conversation, a dialogue with the defendant?" he asked.

"Yes. She called one night, around 5:30. She was screaming at me to put him on the phone. I told her he wasn't home and I hung up."

"Did she call back?" Kelly asked.

"Yes. She kept calling, demanding to speak to him. I kept hanging up." Christina paused. She sat very still, her lips tight, pressed together in a way that made me think of my mother.

Kelly went on. "Mrs. Wheatley," he said softly. "Can you tell us what happened next?"

She took a deep breath. "She called again. She was screaming at me . . . that I'd be sorry if I didn't put him on the phone. That she would ruin him. That I could kiss my beautiful home and comfortable life good-bye. That I should keep close watch on Samantha and Margot."

Christina Wheatley paused again. Then she looked straight at the jury, her lower lip quivering. "She said by the time she was finished, we would have nothing." She pressed her fist against her lips.

"Have you received phone calls since then?" asked Kelly.

"The calls never stopped. I started leaving the phone off the hook. Then she switched to calling Samantha's phone."

"Thank you, Mrs. Wheatley. That will be all for now," Kelly said.

Douglas Newton got up and walked over to Christina Wheatley. "Mrs. Wheatley, in these many phone calls you allege you received from Miss Strickland, did she ever once identify herself?"

"No, not by name," said Christina Wheatley.

"Can you prove that any of the hang-up calls were made by her?" he asked.

"No."

"Can you prove that the taped messages were left by her?"

"No."

"Mrs. Wheatley, you have conveyed to the court that you received numerous unwanted phone calls at all hours of the day and night, that you and your children were threatened. I'm wondering if you took any deliberate action to prevent it from continuing?" asked Newton.

"We saw a lawyer. He said we could press charges. Or we could do nothing and hope it would stop," she said.

"What did you do?" he asked.

"Nothing. We hoped it would stop."

"Interesting choice," he said, his voice tinged with irony. "No more questions."

"Redirect, your honor," Fred Kelly was on his feet.

"Proceed, Mr. Kelly," said the judge.

"Mrs. Wheatley, why did you choose not to do anything?" Kelly asked.

"Because, Mr. Kelly, we thought it would be too damaging for our family to be in the middle of a public scandal," she said.

"Tell us why you are here now," he said.

"Uh . . . well . . . because one evening two detectives rang our doorbell. They came to question Michael. They . . . um . . . told us that Vanessa Strickland had filed criminal charges against him, harassment, stalking and . . . uh . . . something else, I can't remember now," she said. "At that point, we didn't seem to have a choice."

"Thank you, Mrs. Wheatley," said Kelly.

*   *   *

The trial adjourned for the lunch recess. As the courtroom emptied, I watched my father staring straight ahead, his face slack and lethargic. Drained, I made no effort to move.

Finally I said, "This is awful. I don't know how much more I can listen to."

He shook his head. We watched Vanessa and her lawyer walk once again through the door marked **Authorized Personnel**.

"Grace," my father said with sudden energy, his eyes still on the door. "I'm going to talk to them. You want to come?"

I didn't know if I did or not, but I got up and followed him through the doorway. Vanessa and her lawyer sat at a table in one of several windowless rooms in the area. With me at his heels, my father walked in without knocking.

He slipped into a chair across from Vanessa, nodding to Douglas Newton. I waited near the door.

"Vanessa," my father said, facing her. Then he stopped, as if he had forgotten what he wanted to say. She looked down at a legal pad on the table.

"Vanessa," he said again, this time with uncharacteristic sharpness. Startled, she looked up. Then softer, "Help me to understand this. I want to understand," he said, leaning toward her.

"What?" Her eyes widened.

"What you did to these people," he said.

Her face flushed, her mouth dropped open. "What I did to them? How can you ask me that?"

Suddenly the room seemed very quiet, a whirring fan in the corner making the only sound.

"How can you say that to me? You have no idea what that man did to me!" Her voice was shrill, filled with outrage.

Then my father, slowly, his voice now very low, "But you went after them. Not him. You got your revenge on his wife and children."

"Mr. Strickland," interrupted Douglas Newton. "This is not helpful. Right now, Vanessa needs to focus."

My father waved him off.

Vanessa covered her face with her hands and started to cry. Then, in a voice broken with sobs, "I can't believe it, Daddy. You—of all people—turning against me."

My father sat for a minute, first looking at Vanessa, then nowhere in particular. Finally, pushing his chair back from the table, he said: "Come on, Grace. Let's get some lunch."

*   *   *

That evening I went to my mother's for dinner. Six years earlier, she had moved from the house on Wentworth Street into a condominium in the Flushing section of Queens. She had finished her degree in social work and now worked in a mental health clinic several blocks from her apartment. My mother, the mental health worker. I had to laugh. Vanessa said she guessed they'd hire anybody.

My mother still volunteered at what was now the Frederick Levy Bereavement Center. Two evenings a week, she answered the phones and talked to the incoming parents, new arrivals at the center. I met her there a few times over the years and together we would walk the few blocks to her favorite Korean restaurant on Union Street.

But on this night, we sat at her dining room table eating roasted chicken and string beans. She was talking about Herb, her former group dynamics professor at Queens College, whom she had been seeing for years. She was still a pretty woman, even now in her early sixties. She wore her hair, mostly gray, pulled back into a bun. Large tortoise shell glasses drew attention to her face, softer than I remembered it . . . and more relaxed. Her easy smile disconcerted me, a jolting contrast from the image scorched into my memory of a younger, teeth-clenching Margaret, her jaw set in anger.

"Herb's daughter Darlene has month-old twins, so we took a drive to Poughkeepsie to see them. They're just adorable, Grace. So tiny."

I dropped my fork and stared at her.

"Is something wrong?" she asked.

"I don't know . . . this is so messed up. Vanessa's on trial—god knows when you saw her last—and you're visiting Herb's grandchildren! I mean . . . does that make any sense to you?"

She looked down at her plate, her fork toying with the string beans. "It's not that simple," she said, barely above a whisper.

"I guess not." I made no effort to keep the sarcasm out of my voice.

Neither one of us attempted to break through the brittle silence that hovered for the remainder of the meal. After several minutes, I stood up.

"I have to go," I said. I carried my dishes into the kitchen, grabbed my coat and walked to the door. "Thanks for dinner." Not waiting for a response, I let the door close behind me and walked to the elevator.

Seconds later her door creaked open. "Grace." She stepped into the hall. "Please don't leave." she said nervously.

I turned around to face her and saw her hand still clutching the dinner napkin.

"What?" I said, annoyed.

"Come back in . . . please." She looked vulnerable, almost fragile standing in the doorway, her napkin pressed against her mouth.

I hesitated before walking back into her apartment. We sat down facing each other in the matching gold brocade wing chairs, relics from Wentworth Street. Her mouth twitched nervously as she struggled to find words.

"You're angry," she said. "Tell me why?" Her social work training had kicked in.

I took my time answering. "You know . . . every day Dad and I are in that courtroom with Vanessa. And where are you? Apparently visiting Herb's grandchildren."

"Grace, you know Vanessa hates me. She's always hated me. I'm sure she doesn't even want me there."

"And why is that?" My tone insistent, sarcastic.

Shaking her head, she looked away.

"Was she born hating you?" I demanded. "Did she hate you when she was a year old? You were her mother!" My voice had escalated to a shout.

She started to cough and raised the napkin to her mouth. "I see . . . you think I'm the villain, Grace," she said, grasping the napkin. "Vanessa . . . and your father . . . it was . . . they were united against me." She twisted the napkin with both hands and pieces fell to the floor at her feet. The phone started to ring but she didn't get up to answer it.

"The truth is," I began, my voice now softer, "that you opted out. All those years of volunteering to help other people, three, four times a week—while you ignored your own children. That is . . . one of us you ignored. The other one you were downright mean to." I clasped my own trembling hands together between my knees. Somehow I'd finally dredged up the courage to confront my mother.

She looked like she had been slapped, her face red, her mouth open. "I didn't ignore you, Grace. I loved you."

"How can you say that?" I almost bolted out of my chair. "You would go for days without talking to us, giving us the silent treatment. Me included. You never knew anything about my life. You never asked. Never once! That time I tried to tell you Erin had disappeared, you didn't even bother to take your eyes off the newspaper!"

I could see tears beginning to pool above her lashes, but that didn't stop me. I took a deep breath and kept going. "Let's talk about all those letters Erin wrote that you couldn't manage to forward to me. And you think you didn't ignore me! You are so wrapped up in yourself . . . you don't have a clue. You just keep muddling along, making up your own version of reality."

She sat without moving, her eyes closed, her hands clutching the arms of her chair. Bits of the shredded napkin lay in her lap. I sat back in my own chair and watched her, my heart thumping with adrenaline. We'd crossed a new line and I didn't know what lurked on the other side. How would we go on after this? Minutes passed. "It's getting late. I have to get home."

When she opened her eyes, I saw the creases lining her forehead. She cleared her throat. "Is it too late? Can you find a way to forgive me?"

I shrugged. "What does it matter?"

"You're all I have left," she said, her face heavy, defeated.

"That's not true," I snapped back. "You have Herb and his grandchildren."

She flinched. "Grace, why are you saying all this now?"

I picked at a loose thread on the arm of the chair. Even though I could feel her watching me, I kept my eyes averted. "It made me so angry . . . the idea of you visiting Herb's daughter. Especially now . . . during the trial. You abandoned us . . . our whole lives. Mostly Vanessa, but me too. How can you expect to be forgiven for that?"

"I know I've made mistakes," she said slowly, "but I'm asking you to give me another chance. I'd like to start over."

"Start over? What are you thinking? I've spent too many of my 30 years trying to compensate for the lack of you. Because I **never had** a warm, loving mother. There's no starting over for me." The heat of my words lingered like acrid fumes in the air.

I stopped talking, stunned by my own recklessness. I tried to steady my hands and bent over to re-tie my sneakers. I couldn't bring myself to look at her and see some pathetic expression on her face. And, I could barely admit to myself, part of me was still afraid of her.

"I need to go now," I said, glancing up at her.

*   *   *

The following afternoon, Fred Kelly called Michael Wheatley to the stand. Looking younger than his 45 years, he had an almost boyish face with blue eyes and close-cropped sandy colored hair. Samantha looked exactly like him.

Slowly, he told his story. He and Vanessa had met fourteen months earlier when, one morning, he helped her extract her coat from the revolving door at the entrance of their office building. The following week, they ran into each other at the corner coffee shop where he was ordering his coffee, black with one sugar. The next morning she delivered to his office a large black coffee and one packet of sugar. So began their flirtation. Within a few weeks, they had progressed to lunch, then to a drink after work and, ultimately, to sex.

For two hours, he answered Kelly's questions, laying the foundation, brick by brick, of desire run amok. In a voice at times edged with barely concealed anger, he gave life and color to the details alluded to in his wife's earlier testimony, of the gifts, the romantic dinners, the wild weekend getaway, the deceit, the betrayal and, finally, the raw, unimaginable and unmanageable exposure.

I watched him closely, his gestures, the occasional hint of defeat in his rounded shoulders, the bafflement in his eyes. Of all of Vanessa's boyfriends, he was the only one I had actually seen, with the exception of Peter Vanelli back in high school. If he was going for sympathy, he certainly didn't have mine. A willing participant, he had recklessly exposed his family to Vanessa's vindictiveness. As far as I was concerned, he was no better than she.

At 3:30 p.m., the trial was recessed until the following day when Michael Wheatley, still under oath, was back on the stand.

"Mr. Wheatley," said Fred Kelly, "please tell the court why you decided to end your relationship with Vanessa Strickland."

"Well," he began, "in the beginning, I was completely caught up in it. It was exciting . . . exhilarating, I guess you could say. But then it changed."

"Can you be more precise about what changed?" asked Kelly.

"Um . . . well . . . Vanessa got more demanding. She wanted things I couldn't give her . . . like spending more time with her. More weekend trips. She was dissatisfied with the limits. It became a burden."

"What happened when you tried to cut off the relationship?" Kelly asked.

"Vanessa got hysterical. She was furious. She started throwing things. We were in my office late one night—she grabbed a paper weight my daughter Margot had made and threw it at me. She was screaming and cursing, threatening me."

"What threats did she make?" asked Kelly.

"She said she was going to tell my wife and send her pictures of us. And she would go to my boss and tell him I had coerced her into having sex by threatening to have her fired." He stopped, red-faced, out-of-breath.

"Was there any truth in that? Did you coerce her?" asked Kelly.

"Of course not!" he said, emphatically.

"Did you threaten to fire her?" Kelly continued.

"No! I couldn't fire Vanessa," Michael Wheatley said. "She worked in acquisitions. I wasn't even her boss."

"What happened after that?" Kelly asked.

"I thought if I ended it gradually . . . you know . . . uh . . . at a slower pace, it might be easier for her to accept."

He pulled a handkerchief from his pocket and patted his forehead. I could see the perspiration from where I sat some thirty feet away. "So I told her we could see each other, but not as often."

"Did that strategy work?" asked Kelly.

"Initially," said Michael Wheatley. "The next day she apologized. She said she was ashamed of the things she'd said, that it would never happen again. But it did—a few days later, it happened again. After that, it was a roller coaster. I never knew which Vanessa I'd be dealing with."

"Mr. Wheatley, on the police record, you charged Ms. Strickland with harassment, extortion and stalking. Please tell the jury exactly why you made these charges," said Kelly.

"Well, she called my home several times a day . . . and my office constantly. She followed me to meetings. To lunch. She waited outside for me after work. She left notes with the doorman at my apartment building. She even took a note to Samantha at her school."

"What did you do in response?" Kelly asked.

"At first, I tried reasoning with her. Then I decided to ignore her. I stopped taking her phone calls. Whenever I saw her, I just nodded in her direction and kept moving. That infuriated her. Then she started blackmailing me."

"What, specifically, did she want?" asked Kelly.

"The list kept growing. It started with jewelry. She wanted several pieces of jewelry. She wanted me to pay for her vacation to Hawaii. She wanted me to go with her to her mother's house and pretend to be her fiancé."

I bolted forward in my chair, blinking in disbelief. Where had that come from? I turned to my father. He was shaking his head. I couldn't believe Vanessa had actually said that. What did she want? Margaret's approval? Revenge of some sort?

"Did you agree to any of these demands?" asked Kelly.

"I told her I'd buy her one piece of jewelry. She picked a ring for $3,600. I said it was too much. Then she threatened to go to my boss." He was shaking his head, his flushed face dotted with sweat.

"Did you purchase the ring for her?" asked Kelly.

"No," he said. "I didn't. I began to think it would never end, that I couldn't buy her cooperation with one piece of jewelry. She was too unpredictable. At the same time she was begging me to stay with her, she was also calling my home and leaving these awful messages for my wife to hear. And my daughter. My god, she—Vanessa—she has no conscience . . ."

Oh! And you have one? I shook my head in disgust at his hypocrisy . . . even though he definitely had a point. I had often wondered why Vanessa never seemed remorseful for things she had done, deliberately done, to hurt people. Michael looked at me for a moment although I'm sure he didn't know who I was.

I glanced over at Vanessa. She sat impassively, her hands folded on the table in front of her, her face blank, revealing nothing. What drove her? I remembered myself, seven years old, walking home from school with her, turning to see Suzanne Springer carrying the slashed pieces of her prize-winning felt turkey. Nobody else was allowed to have the things Vanessa wanted. She made sure of that.

"Objection!" thundered Douglas Newton.

"Sustained," said the judge. "The last statement will be stricken from the record."

"Mr. Wheatley, did the defendant carry out the threats she made to you?" Kelly asked.

Michael Wheatley took a deep breath. "Yes. Every single one of them. And more. She told my wife . . . and my children. She called my boss and complained of sexual harassment. She went to the police and pressed criminal charges. **FALSE** charges."

"What consequences have you suffered as a result?" asked Kelly.

Michael Wheatley reached up and raked his finger through his hair. "My wife Christina and I separated. Three months ago. My daughter Samantha won't speak to me. Margot is the only one who will see me. At work . . . people get very quiet when I walk into the room. They start whispering when I leave. Most of them avoid me. I've lost a lot of credibility." His voice was flat, defeated.

My father and I looked at each other. "I don't blame his wife for leaving him," I whispered. "He's as much to blame as Vanessa."

My father shrugged. Was he thinking about his own infidelity? I wondered.

"Are you still employed at the Ameri-Zone Corporation?" asked Kelly.

"Yes, so far I am," he said. "I . . . um . . . I saved the tapes—you know—the messages she left on my answering machine. When she began threatening me, I started taping our phone conversations. The tapes prove our relationship was consensual."

"Thank you, Mr. Wheatley. No more questions for now," said Kelly.

Douglas Newton got up and walked over to the jury box. "Mr. Wheatley, isn't it true that you initiated the relationship between Miss Strickland and yourself?"

Michael Wheatley hesitated. "We flirted with each other. It was mutual."

"Didn't you invite Miss Strickland to lunch?" asked Newton.

"Yes."

"So, you don't deny being the aggressor?" continued Newton.

"Yes, I deny it. An invitation to lunch is hardly an act of aggression," he shot back.

Newton ignored the response. "In fact, Mr. Wheatley, you have quite a reputation as a ladies' man at Ameri-Zone, don't you?"

"Objection," said Kelly.

"Sustained," said the judge.

"Mr. Wheatley, isn't it true that it was Miss Strickland who wanted to end the relationship?" asked Newton.

"No. That is not true," said Mr. Wheatley.

"Isn't it true that you threatened to have her fired if she left you?" Newton went on.

"Absolutely not. I just said Vanessa did not work for me."

"Who did Miss Strickland work for?" asked Newton.

"Charles Grund."

"Isn't Charles Grund a close friend of yours?" asked Newton.

"We're colleagues," said Mr. Wheatley. "We are not close friends."

Douglas Newton walked over to the witness. "Didn't you just play golf with Charles Grund earlier this month?" he asked, almost smirking.

"It was a large group outing," said Mr. Wheatley.

"Was that an affirmative response, Mr. Wheatley?" asked Newton.

"Yes."

"Tell me, Mr. Wheatley, does Vanessa Strickland still work at Ameri-Zone?" asked Newton.

"No."

"Did she resign her position?" he continued.

"No."

"Was she fired?" asked Newton.

"Yes, but . . ."

"That will be all, Mr. Wheatley," said Newton. "I have no more questions of this witness, your honor."

"Mr. Kelly?" said the judge.

"The State rests, your honor," said Kelly.

"Then we are adjourned until tomorrow at 10:00 a.m.," said the judge.

I sat back in my seat and watched Vanessa. My father told me she'd be testifying next. It didn't seem possible for her to overcome all the testimony. Especially Samantha's. Part of me wanted to see her punished for what she had done. To see this jury do what neither of my parents had. But . . . jail? I couldn't go that far.

*   *   *

The next morning, Douglas Newton called Vanessa to testify. She got up slowly, smiling modestly at the jury as she made her way to the witness chair. She managed to avoid looking at us, no doubt an intentional slight—her pay-back for the day my father had demanded an explanation. Exasperated, I glared at her, willing her to acknowledge us.

Vanessa's austere appearance, absent make-up and jewelry, seemed calculated to suggest simplicity and perhaps, by extension, innocence. Her hair drawn back off her face exposed her smooth, clear skin and enviable features. The slight scar on her upper lip, the only visible imperfection. She looked calm and in control, an emphatic contradiction of Michael Wheatley's portrayal. She must be on tranquilizers, I thought.

Vanessa's version of the onset of their relationship matched Michael Wheatley's, except for her insistence on his role as the aggressor. Led by Douglas Newton's questions, she painted a picture of a man often heavy-handed in his pursuit of her, who refused to hear "no" as an answer and demonstrated the intent to have a relationship with her at any cost. He seduced her with candle-lit dinners, expensive gifts, promises to advance her career, a weekend at a charming country inn and a pervasive, all-consuming attentiveness.

"Vanessa, what led you to end your relationship with Mr. Wheatley?" asked Newton.

"Well, I . . . Michael began talking about leaving his wife so that we could be together," said Vanessa, her eyes fixed on her lawyer. Her voice was tight, brittle. Despite the seemingly serene exterior, I could see she was nervous.

"You didn't want him to leave his wife?" Newton continued.

"I . . . well . . . I'm not sure. I mean . . . yes, I did . . . I wanted it very much. At the same time, I felt guilty. I kept thinking about his family. I knew what we were doing was a sin," Vanessa said, lowering her gaze to her lap, to her folded hands. She reached up with her left hand and pushed a few strands of hair from her face.

I watched her closely. She was performing, manipulating the jury. Guilt? Sin? I almost laughed.

"What did you do?" asked Newton.

Vanessa looked up at her lawyer. "I didn't know what to do. I agonized over it. I lost a lot of sleep. Finally, I went to my mother and told her everything. She helped me understand that I needed to stop seeing Michael." Again she lowered her eyes.

Wow. She's good, I thought to myself.

I felt my father's body tense. I held my breath. Neither one of us moved, not even to look at each other. We knew Margaret was the last person Vanessa would ever seek out. I glanced at the jury. They were all watching her, leaning forward to hear her. She was getting to them.

"Did you tell Mr. Wheatley what you had decided?" asked Newton.

"Yes."

"How did he react?"

"At first, he tried to talk me out of it. He said we loved each other, we needed to be together, we deserved to be together," she said. "When he realized that I was determined to end it, he got angry."

"How did he express this anger?" asked Newton.

"He threatened me. He told me he would have me fired, that he would put the word out to other companies not to hire me. He said he would use all of his power and influence to disrupt my career."

"Please tell the court what position you held at the Ameri-zone Corporation," Douglas Newton interjected.

"Administrative assistant to the vice president of acquisitions," Vanessa said.

"Now, getting back to your conversation with Michael Wheatley. What did you do when he threatened to 'disrupt your career'?"

"I was terrified," Vanessa said, glancing wide-eyed at the jury. "I didn't know what to do. I continued to see him. I was afraid to stop. I tried to make myself undesirable so he'd want to stop seeing me. I acted like I was crazy. I cried a lot. I pretended to be out of control."

She's unbelievably clever, I thought. If I didn't know her so well, I might actually believe her.

"Was this successful?" asked Newton.

"Over a period of time. Yes, it was. I could see he was losing patience with me, so I kept it up," said Vanessa. "Then one day, he said he needed to talk to me, that he had a proposition for me. He said he would let me go if I helped him break up his marriage. He told me his wife had refused for years to give him a divorce, and he wanted me to 'push her over the edge'—those were his exact words—so she'd want to be rid of him . . . so she'd let him go."

"What exactly did he want you to do?" asked Newton.

"He had a plan all laid out," said Vanessa. "He wanted me to make phone calls to his house—hundreds of phone calls. Day and night. In the initial phase of the plan, I would simply call and hang up."

"What came next, after the initial phase?" asked Newton.

"Then I was to call and leave messages on the answering machine. Messages about us . . . for his wife to hear. About how we had great sex, how he gave me gifts and took me away for the weekend. Things like that," she said.

Oh my god. Who thought of this? I looked over at the jury. Are they believing it?

"And the next phase?" Newton queried.

"He made recordings of his own voice, saying things like—I can't wait to see you and I think about you all the time. I was supposed to play these tapes onto the answering machine at his house."

"Was that all?" asked Newton.

"No," replied Vanessa. "The final thing was for me to deliver the note to Samantha at her school. He thought Christina would go ballistic when she found out about that."

"Vanessa, I'm sure there are people here in the court room who feel you did some terrible things," said Newton. "How would you explain your actions to them?"

Vanessa hesitated before looking apologetically at the jury. "That man—Michael Wheatley—was holding me hostage. He was threatening to ruin my career. Listen . . . I felt awful about doing some of those things. But . . . I just wanted my life back." She put her face in her hands and shook her head. Then she turned toward her lawyer. "It was what I had to do to get my life back."

"Thank you, Vanessa," said Newton. "I have no more questions."

Fred Kelly stood and walked briskly to the witness stand. "Miss Strickland," he began. "Do you have a single shred of evidence to support your statement that Michael Wheatley orchestrated these phone calls in the manner you have described?"

"No," she said, looking at Kelly. She sat up suddenly, her eyes darting to the back of the courtroom. I followed her gaze in time to see what looked like my mother pushing her way out through the swinging door.

"No?" he asked, incredulous.

I elbowed my father. "Mom was here. She just walked out," I whispered.

She must've heard Vanessa saying, only a few minutes ago, that she'd gone to her mother for help. Of all the days she could've come, she picked this one. I shook my head and almost chuckled out loud at the irony.

"I'm sorry," Vanessa faltered. "What was the question?" A red flush had filled her face. She took a long deep breath.

"The witness has already answered, your honor," Newton said, cutting her off.

"Move on, Mr. Kelly," said the judge.

"Miss Strickland, what about the tapes you claim Michael Wheatley made, the ones you recorded on his wife's answering machine? Surely you must have those tapes," Kelly said.

"No, I don't," said Vanessa. "I returned them to Michael. He wanted them back."

"Didn't you think it might be important for you to keep those tapes?" asked Kelly.

Vanessa's facial expression never changed though her voice revealed a hint of hostility. "I certainly never imagined that a love affair would lead to a criminal trial, Mr. Kelly. Unlike your client, I didn't anticipate the need for evidence."

"Just yes or no, Miss Strickland," said Kelly.

"No," said Vanessa.

Fred Kelly turned around and retrieved a note pad from his table. Flipping through a few pages, he walked back toward the witness stand.

"Miss Strickland, the supervisor from NYNEX, Mr. Davis, testified that you made 442 calls from your office to the office of Michael Wheatley. Were these calls also part of his so-called plan?"

Vanessa shifted in the chair. "No," she said.

"How, then, can you explain this . . . . staggering number of phone calls?" asked Kelly.

"I was involved in a relationship with Michael Wheatley. I called him often. And he called me often," Vanessa said.

"Miss Strickland, why did you make those eighteen calls to his daughter Samantha?" asked Kelly.

Vanessa hesitated. "It was part of his plan," she said, her eyes shifting to Douglas Newton.

"Really?" asked Kelly. "You didn't mention it when you were describing the different phases, to use your word, of Mr. Wheatley's plan."

"It was part of his plan," Vanessa repeated, sounding less confident.

"Do you really expect the jury to believe that Michael Wheatley wanted to alienate his own daughter?" asked Kelly.

"It was a way to upset his wife," replied Vanessa.

"Did he tell you to call Samantha between the hours of 3:00 and 5:00 a.m.? Or did you pick those times yourself?" Kelly demanded.

"Throughout this entire period, I followed Michael's explicit instructions," said Vanessa.

"I don't believe you answered my question," said Kelly.

"He picked the times."

"So, in addition to getting rid of his wife, he wanted you to disrupt his daughter's sleep on eighteen different occasions?" Fred Kelly's voice, replete with sarcasm.

"Objection!" Douglas Newton was on his feet.

"Withdrawn," said Kelly, returning to his chair. "I have no more questions of this witness."

"Mr. Newton, please call your next witness," the judge said.

The defense rests, your honor," said Newton.

"Then we'll hear closing arguments in the morning," said the judge.

My father and I lingered in our seats while the court room emptied. What was he thinking? It had been a dazzling performance. She had every answer ready. And my mother! Had I shamed her into coming? My head was reeling.

When everyone else was gone, we got up to leave. At the door, my father turned to me and said: "Grace, look . . . over there."

My eyes followed his gesture to the wall across from the courtroom. Standing there, alone, a slender woman with red hair and freckles. My mouth fell open. Slowly, I raised my hand to cover it.

"Erin?" I whispered.

She took a small step toward me before hesitating. Tentatively, I walked over to her. My sudden tears blurred her face. I felt her take my hand.

"How did you know where to find me?" I asked.

"Miss Zrinsky told me," she said. "Let's go outside."

We walked out and down the courthouse steps. Awkwardness had edged its way in, hovering around us. I sifted through my thoughts trying to come up with some way to ease the re-entry. We had been too close to be casual, but now . . . in some respects, we were almost strangers.

"Erin," I began, searching for the words to make it right. "I'm sorry . . . . I feel terrible . . . I just dropped out of your life."

She looked at me but said nothing.

I struggled against a growing sense of futility. Eventually, I began again. "I wanted to be there for you . . . you were always there for me . . . always. I just really didn't know how to deal with what happened to you."

We sat down on a bench, Erin staring out at the river. Still she said nothing. She lowered her eyes and began playing with the ring on her finger.

"Each time I sat down to write you a letter, I didn't know what to say. It felt wrong to talk about myself and all the fun I was having at Syracuse . . . considering what you were going through." My voice trailed off.

We sat, again in silence. Finally I said, "I don't know what you think about me now . . . but you should know it took me years to get over losing you. I needed you . . . I honestly didn't even know how to live without you." I pulled a tissue from my purse and blew my nose. "You were the only person in my life I could count on. You and Miss Zrinsky."

Erin slowly turned to face me. "You know, Grace . . . neither one of us is perfect. I felt pretty awful about not answering your letters when your father was offering me a place to live." She sat back and looked out at the river. "Maybe we should try to . . . just go on from here."

We both got quiet again as I took this in. Minutes passed.

"You saw Miss Zrinsky?" I asked, finally.

She shook her head. "I talked to her on the phone. I told her I was coming in for my grandmother's funeral."

"Did Calvin come with you?" I asked.

"No. I came with my mother . . . and my brothers and sisters. It's the first trip back for all of us."

"How is your mother?"

"Pretty good," said Erin. "She's remarried now. And we've all grown up. Everyone except Timmy. He's a senior in high school. He lives with her and her husband in Omaha."

"And your father?"

"He's still in prison," she said, looking out at the water. "He's serving a 60-year-sentence. Child sexual abuse carries heavy penalties. In addition to the other charges." Our eyes met briefly. Then she looked away.

"Oh god, Erin. All those years . . . I never had any idea," I whispered.

"Well," she said, raising her eyes to meet mine. "He's getting what he deserves now. Almost."

"What about Calvin?"

"We're still together. He's been good for me. He's solid and honorable. From my perspective, that's saying a lot. Our daughter, Mary Therese—we call her Tracey—will be twelve on her next birthday. She's a terrific kid."

"Do you have other children?"

"No," said Erin, quickly. "I didn't want more children. Every time my family had to split up, I felt like someone had ripped the limbs from my body."

"Do you still live in the apartment over his parents' garage?"

Erin laughed. "No, we have our own house now. But we aren't far from Calvin's parents. I'm very close to his mother. She really helped me hold things together when I barely had the energy to get up in the morning. I named Mary Therese after her."

"What about you, Erin?"

She smiled. "I'm in school. A bona fide college student, at long last," she said, twirling her ring again. "It's your turn now. I've been doing all the talking."

"Oh . . . I don't know . . . right now I'm feeling . . . out-of-sync, I guess. After college, I was going to go for a master's in psychology, maybe even a doctorate, but I started to work and never really got back to it. For the past few years, I've been working as a recruiter at American Express. It's pretty interesting, actually. Last month, I was looking to find candidates for a marketing manager position. In one month, I flew to Dallas, Seattle and San Diego to interview people. I took a few extra days in Seattle to spend some time there with a friend from college.

"Anyway . . . I've been thinking lately about what my next step should be. If I get promoted in HR—is that even what I want? I have a lot to figure out."

"Several years ago, Miss Zrinsky told me you had a serious boyfriend. What happened to him?"

"Oh, really? Have you and Miss Zrinsky stayed in contact all these years?"

"Yeah, we have. I call her every few months," Erin said.

"Oh. I'm surprised. I mean . . . Ms. Zrinsky never said anything." I bit my lip to keep from asking Erin why she hadn't called me. It was my fault, I knew.

"You were going to tell me about the boyfriend," Erin said.

"Oh, yes. That must've been Paul. For awhile I thought we'd get married." I hesitated. "It's strange to be talking about this now. I've been thinking about him a lot lately . . . since the trial began." Suddenly uncomfortable, I stood up to stretch my legs.

"Is this a bad subject?" Erin asked. She pushed her hair off her face, the red hair that had always signaled her arrival even before her face was visible. I used to find stray red hairs on my clothing.

"No . . . not any more. It's been almost four years, practically ancient history," I said. "But when it first ended, it was . . . seismic. I struggled over it for at least a year."

"How did you meet?"

"On the subway. The #2 train. We kept seeing each other on the morning commute and eventually started smiling in recognition. One morning he followed me off the train, and we met for a drink later that week. Within a year, we were living together." I hesitated, surprised to hear my voice wavering. I took a deep breath.

Erin reached over and put her hand on my shoulder. "I thought he was the one," I whispered.

"What happened?" Her voice gentle, just the way I'd remembered it.

"Well . . . uh . . . this is not a good story. Paul was out of work for about a month . . . you know, between jobs. One afternoon, I was at a meeting that wrapped up early so I went home to surprise him. You'll never guess who was there. Vanessa. I didn't catch them doing anything. I mean . . . they were just sitting in the living room talking, but they both looked so shocked when I walked in. Like they had something to hide. I couldn't believe she was there. I still wince at the memory of myself frozen in the doorway, wanting to turn and run.

"She ended up leaving pretty quickly. But I couldn't shake the feeling that something had been going on. I mean . . . why else would she have been there? It destroyed our relationship."

"Your relationship with Vanessa?" Erin asked.

I took a deep breath. My throat felt parched. "No. My relationship with Paul. Every time I looked at him, I thought of it. Nothing between us was good after that. It had to end."

"God, Grace. I can't believe her."

"Yeah, me either. There's nothing honorable about Vanessa. Like the man in the courtroom just said, she has no conscience."

Erin frowned. "How come you're going to the trial?" she asked. "She doesn't deserve your loyalty."

"I went for my father. So he wouldn't have to be there alone. On top of everything else, my grandmother died a few months ago. It's been tough for him."

"I'm sorry to hear that," she said. "What's the story with Vanessa?"

"I really don't get it. She keeps getting herself involved in one bad situation after another. She finds these unavailable men and becomes obsessed with them. She loses herself in the reckless pursuit of these relationships. It's impossible to talk to her or reason with her when it's happening. I've tried. Many times."

"What does she say?" Erin asked.

"She's completely irrational. You'd have to see it to believe it. Everything that happens is always someone else's fault." I kicked my shoe off and tapped it on the pavement to dislodge a pebble.

"Remember that boyfriend she had when she was in college?" I asked. Erin nodded.

"He was the first. At least the first one I knew about. Vanessa messed herself up over him . . . it was unimaginable. She harassed him, stalked him really, until he finally had her arrested. The case was eventually plea-bargained. My father paid the fine for her but she had to perform something like 50 hours of community service. After that, she never went back to school."

"My god," Erin said. "I had no idea. Miss Zrinsky never said anything."

"It's hard to remember now . . . but I think that happened just after you left. I was in my first year of college when she was finally arrested.

"It didn't end there either," I continued. "Although I wasn't involved with it while I was in college, but once or twice she came to stay with me to escape whatever mess she was in. I don't think she has any friends. I can't remember the last time she introduced me to a friend. Well, it's not surprising. She has nothing to give."

"Where does she work?" Erin asked.

"Right now she's not working. She was fired over the mess that led to this trial. Before that, she was an administrative assistant at a pharmaceutical company. She had trouble on that job too," I went on. "She got involved with some married man and started calling his wife. At least that one didn't end up in court. I used to feel sorry for her. Then, of course, after Paul . . . my capacity for sympathy diminished substantially. But my father . . . her behavior torments him. He asked me last week if I thought my mother had been right, that he was responsible for the way Vanessa turned out."

"Really?" Erin seemed surprised.

"Yeah," I said. "I must say . . . I've had the same thought myself. Somehow . . . he was always there to intercede for her, so she never had to deal with her own consequences." I drew my feet up, Indian-style, on the bench.

"But your father . . ." Erin said softly. "He's such a kind man. Vanessa gets her meanness somewhere else."

I wasn't ready to talk about my ambivalence toward my father. I sat back and stretched my arms behind my head.

"I guess my father must look like a saint to you, Erin," I said. "After everything you've been through."

She didn't respond.

"How come you never told me about your father?"

"I didn't know how to," she said simply. "I was too ashamed."

"Did he molest you?"

She nodded.

"Did he molest all six of you?"

We both sat very still. Every inconsequential noise around us seemed magnified.

"Three of us. The three oldest," Erin said, staring out at the water.

"Did you talk about it . . . at least to each other?"

"No. I thought it was only me. We each thought that, at least while it was happening. We found out the truth later. After he was arrested."

"When did it start?" I asked.

"When I was eight."

Eight! I shook my head. "Erin, why didn't you tell me? Maybe I could've helped you."

"It doesn't work that way, Grace." It's way too complicated to be that easy."

I wasn't sure what she meant but decided not to say anything.

Finally, I began. "You know, over the years, I've thought a lot about that day at the street fair when we saw my father. You know . . . with that woman."

I watched Erin's expression change, as she remembered it herself. I went on. "What I think about is how you helped me, how you tried to keep me from seeing him. You held onto me, the whole way back to Queens, you were right there next to me. I've never helped you like that."

"Yes, you have," Erin said. "You've helped me in a hundred different ways."

"Not in like kind," I said.

Erin laughed. "In like kind? Where did you come up with that?"

I shrugged, smiling at her.

Finally Erin stood and stretched her back. "Let's go take Miss Zrinsky to dinner," she said, looking down at me. "I told her I'd try to get to the library before closing. It'll take us 45 minutes to get to Queens."

I got up and we began walking toward the subway. "Grace, is there a man in your life now?" Erin asked.

"No. Nobody significant."

"Has there been anyone since Paul?"

"Nothing that's lasted more than a few months. I don't know . . . being in a relationship . . . I guess I'm not very good at it. I meet these guys—they're attractive and intelligent—everything looks good in the beginning. But then, after maybe a couple of months, I find out there's an old girlfriend he's going back to . . . or an ex-wife . . . or he's an alcoholic.

"Last year I went out with this guy—Stuart Waites. I met him one Sunday afternoon—walking down Riverside Drive. I saw him coming toward me with a big Golden Retriever. I was eating a muffin, a banana nut muffin. It slipped out of my hand just as they reached me. Well, the dog pounced on my muffin and ate it. So, we laughed—Stuart and I—and started to talk. We met a couple of nights later for a drink. I ended up going out with him for almost four months. Then one night, I was at the bus stop on 79th and Broadway—I see him get into a taxi with a woman. We made eye contact just as he was pulling the door closed. Ten days went by—I didn't hear from him. I finally called him at work. It turns out . . . the woman was his wife. The whole time we were going out, he was living with his wife."

"Do you want to get married, Grace?"

"I don't know. Maybe not. I haven't seen a marriage I'd want for myself. And so many of the men I meet . . . they're so dishonest. Even my own father . . ."

"Are you lonely?"

"Sometimes," I said. "But I have several close friends. Lila—from college—we do a lot of things together. Museums, movies, stuff like that. The past few winters, we rented shares in a ski house in Vermont. And I have friends from work . . . one at American Express and one from Wells, Rich, Green—the advertising agency I used to work for. Oh . . . and I sometimes see Andrea Jaeger. Remember her? She lives a few blocks from me. She's divorced and has a daughter, a three year-old. A couple of weeks ago, we took her daughter to the zoo in Central Park. And last fall we did the Breast Cancer Walk together. Her mother died of breast cancer a couple of years ago. Andrea's having a hard time. She'll be amazed to hear I saw you."

"Did I tell you . . . Miss Zrinsky is Tracey's godmother?" Erin asked.

"No," I said, turning toward Erin. "How did that happen?"

"I wanted to honor her in some way, to thank her for all the things she's done for me. And I wanted Tracey to be connected to her."

I thought about this for a minute. "She must have felt so flattered," I said. "I hope if it had been me, I'd have thought to do the same."

*   *   *

Erin and I sat facing Miss Zrinsky in a booth at the Athenas Diner, one of our old stand-bys on Northern Boulevard.

"It's so good to see you girls together again," she said, smiling at us, her white hair framing her face. "You must be 30 years old now." The deep lines in her face changed with each new expression. She had to be well into her seventies.

"We turned 31 this year." I smiled back at her.

"Miss Zrinsky, I thought you were going to retire," Erin interjected.

"I am mostly retired," she replied. "Grace can tell you. She went to my retirement dinner. I only go in twice a week to help out for part of the day. The library is home to me. I didn't want to leave it entirely."

"What do you do with the rest of your time?" Erin asked.

"Some gardening, some reading. I play Scrabble at the Senior Center," she said. "And I've been helping with a research project for the Holocaust museum . . . the one that's opening in the next year or two."

"A Holocaust museum . . ." my voice trailed off. I looked closely at her, this generous woman whose kindness had eased our adolescent burdens.

"Miss Zrinsky," I cleared my throat. "It's just now occurring to me . . . I've known you for such a long time, but I don't know anything about you. About your life, I mean."

"It wasn't appropriate for you to know about me," she said, looking first at me, then at Erin. "You were young girls helping me in the library."

"Isn't it appropriate now?" asked Erin. I was relieved to see that she hadn't somehow obtained this information without me.

"Tell us about your family," I jumped in.

Stirring her tea, Miss Zrinsky said nothing at first, then looked up at us. "Have you heard of Wolozyn?" she asked. "It's a small town in Poland. I grew up there with my parents and my brother and sister. Everything changed for us when the war started. The Russians . . . they came to our town and stormed into all the houses, forcing the people into the streets. My sister Molly and I hid in the basement, in a crawl space behind the furnace. For nearly two days we stayed there . . . we were afraid to leave. When we finally crawled out, the town was deserted. Later we learned everyone ended up in Chelmno, a concentration camp. My parents and my brother Albert, he was twelve at the time, they were taken too."

"How old were you?" Erin asked.

"Fifteen. Molly was a year older."

"What did you do?" I asked. I tried to imagine myself at fifteen, alone in a deserted place.

"We couldn't stay in Wolozyn. We packed some food and water and began walking. The first night we slept in someone's house. It looked like it had been ransacked because the doors were wide open when we got there."

"Did you know where you were?" Erin asked.

Miss Zrinsky shook her head.

"How did you get away?" I asked.

"A man driving a horse and wagon picked us up as we walked down the road. He hid us under a blanket in the wagon. Another girl was already there . . . under the same blanket. Her name was Frieda." Taking a tissue from her purse, Miss Zrinsky gently blew her nose. "To this day, Frieda is like a sister to me," she said quietly.

I felt a sudden chill and reached for my sweater. "What happened then?" I asked.

"He put the three of us on a train to Vilna. Aleksander. I never forgot his name. He was the first of many strangers who helped us." She took off her glasses and rubbed her eyes.

"And when you got there?" I watched Miss Zrinsky's hands as she held her cup—wrinkled hands, knobby and swollen around her knuckles.

"We went to a rooming house. Frieda's family knew the manager. He took us in and let us stay without paying. We helped with small jobs . . . doing laundry, making beds.

After a few weeks, we were able to get word to our uncles in the United States." Miss Zrinsky stared, almost trance-like, at the table.

"In Wolozyn, my father had been in contact with his three brothers in America. They were saving money to send for us. My father told us—Molly, Albert and me—how we could get in touch with them if anything happened to him. He wrote the information on three small pieces of paper and put them under the insoles in our shoes. I wonder to this day . . . what would've happened to us if he hadn't thought to do this?"

"What did your uncles do?" Erin was leaning on the table toward Miss Zrinsky.

"They sent a cable and told us to stay where we were until we could get documents to leave. So . . . we were stuck in Vilna . . . with refugees everywhere. A typhoid epidemic broke out." Her voice cracked. She patted her mouth with a napkin. Erin and I exchanged nervous glances.

"My sister Molly got sick. We were afraid to be separated so Frieda and I kept her in our room and nursed her. Molly never fully regained her strength. As a child, she had always been sickly. She died within a year of our arrival in the United States . . . just before her eighteenth birthday." Miss Zrinsky raised the napkin to wipe her eyes.

Goose bumps covered both of my arms. I crossed them in front of me, hugging myself, my eyes glued on Miss Zrinsky. Erin, sitting next to me, put her face in her hands. The three of us sat without speaking. How could it be that we hadn't known any of this?

Miss Zrinsky finally broke the silence. "Our uncles sent us money for our passage. For Frieda too. It came to almost two thousand dollars apiece. They scraped and borrowed to do it. This was in 1941, only a few years after they themselves had gone to the United States. They met us at the train station in New York and took us to their home. Frieda came with us. Her entire family was gone."

I stared at Miss Zrinsky, trying to swallow over the lump in my throat. All those years I had spent with her in the library, I had never, not even once, thought to ask her about her life. Erin and I looked at each other. Unwittingly, we had dredged up these memories.

"Miss Zrinsky," I said, whispering. "You lost your whole family . . ."

"Almost," she said. "Several years after the war, Albert and I were reunited. He did not perish in Chelmno, as our parents had. Thankfully, for some unknowable reason, he was spared. And because of the paper my father put into the lining of his shoe, he was able to find our uncles.

"Today I have Albert and Frieda and their families. Frieda lives on Long Island, thirty minutes from here on the train. She has three sons. Albert lives in Queens, just a few blocks from me. He and his wife Rose have one daughter. They named her Molly."

Again, she took off her glasses and rubbed her eyes. "Molly has brought us great joy. Now there are nine grandchildren and six great grandchildren. From rubble, we made a new family."

I couldn't take my eyes off Miss Zrinsky. I was seeing her, really seeing her, for the first time.

"Miss Zrinsky, you never married?" asked Erin.

"No," she smiled.

"I'm embarrassed to remember how we bothered you with our trivial problems," I said. "And you were always so patient."

Miss Zrinsky looked down at her cup, stirring the dregs. She spoke slowly. "Some people think that American children have easy lives. Maybe so. But my own cousins, as teenagers in America, worked all day and went to school at night to help raise money to bring us to the United States."

She leaned forward and looked at us. "I came from a loving family. My mother and father would have done anything for us. Erin was violated by her own father. And you, Grace . . . you suffered as well. Because of your parents. This, to me, is a travesty. I have never thought your problems were trivial.

*   *   *

Slowly, Erin and I walked arm in arm to the subway. "You haven't said anything about your mother," she said.

"It's never been my favorite subject, as you know," I said. "We get together about once a month, usually for dinner, and, to be fair, I'd have to say that things are marginally better between us now. But I still think about what a terrible mother she was . . . so cold and angry all the time. And yet, the people over at the Bereavement Center think she's next in line to Mother Teresa. I mean, some of them really love her. I just don't get it . . . how she has so much to give them . . . and had nothing for us. When Miss Zrinsky was talking, I kept thinking—what a terrible injustice that her family was ripped from her life . . . while my mother simply threw hers away."

I was walking on the beach at Rockaway. The sand was perfectly clean, without the usual array of beer and soda cans, potato chip bags and other trash. Ahead, I saw something glittering. I walked over to it and pulled the shiny object from the sand. It was a gold locket, just like the one my grandmother had given to me.

When I woke up, I remembered back through the years to the awful sinking feeling I'd had the moment I realized the locket was gone. Now, in the wake of my dream, I knew . . . what I'd pulled from the sand was Erin.

Grace

Three months after the trial, I took the subway to Queens and walked toward the eight-story, tan brick apartment building where Vanessa lived. I hadn't seen her since the day she was acquitted and couldn't even remember the last time we'd had a meaningful conversation.

Over time, our relationship had deteriorated to a point dangerously close to unsalvageable. We saw each other a few times a year during our infrequent dinners with my father, for whom we maintained a half-hearted charade. It hadn't always been like this.

After I graduated from college, we got together almost every week, usually for dinner or a movie. On an occasional weekend, we'd go to one of the dance clubs around the city. Her favorite was the Limelight, a huge, stone Gothic-style church packed with lots of trendy young people willing to stand outside for over an hour, sometimes longer, just to get in. Vanessa relished her role as the older sister, clearly proud of herself for knowing all the hip places to go.

My third time there, I met Jim Kartofas, a 31 year old stock broker from Astoria, not far from where I grew up in Queens. I thought he was falling in love with me, the way he called me every day, took me to beautiful restaurants and brought a single long stem rose every time we met. I spent an embarrassing number of hours thinking about him, doodling his name on the notepad next to my computer, taking stock of the latest fashions in wedding attire. My fantasies came to an abrupt end when I called him one night and a woman answered the phone.

Get used to it, Vanessa told me.

I still think about the night we met when, from the dance floor, I had pointed to Vanessa, who was leaning against the bar talking to some guy. "There's my sister." I had to shout to be heard over the music.

"Seriously?" He looked genuinely surprised. "You don't look alike."

"She looks like our mother. I look like my father." I never fared well in these comparisons. Vanessa was startlingly pretty and a full three inches taller than I. I knew I was cute, with my round face and curly brown hair, but next to Vanessa, I felt ordinary.

"You know the guy she's with?" he asked.

I shook my head.

"That's Manny Donadio. He probably supplies 20% of the drugs in this place."

I turned around to look at them. "You mean pot and stuff like that?" I asked.

"You name it, he's got it," he said, grinning.

I glanced back at Vanessa and Manny. Why wouldn't she have told me? I wondered what else she was keeping from me.

But what really alienated me was Vanessa's propensity for creating crises. She'd become involved with a man, usually a married man, and eventually the relationship would sour. The more the man retreated, the more frenetically Vanessa pursued him. I called it the Timothy Hamer syndrome.

She would call me, crying uncontrollably, often in the middle of the night. She became wild, abusive even, the time I suggested she stay away from married men. I was only supposed to sympathize, being too young, too inexperienced and too naïve to presume to know anything she didn't know. It got very old very fast.

One particular night, she was so upset that I told her she could come over even though it was past 2:00 a.m. She never showed up. The next day I called her from work.

"What happened to you last night?" I didn't try to hide my annoyance.

"Oh, Grace. I started to get dressed but I just didn't have the energy to get myself out, so I went back to bed."

"That's it? You just went back to bed?" I was furious.

"Well, I believe that's what I just said," she snapped back.

"That's just great, Vanessa. I've been up since two because you didn't bother to let me know you weren't coming."

"Oh, I get it," she said. "This is all about **YOU** now. Well, you can save the judgemental bullshit for someone else. Sometimes you're just like her, Grace."

"Like who?" A second later, the dial tone buzzed in my ear. I looked at the phone in disbelief. Her voice played back in my head for the rest of the day. "Sometimes you're just like her Grace." I knew who she meant. It was the ultimate insult. We didn't speak to each other again for almost two months.

*   *   *

I took a deep breath and rang the bell next to the name V. Strickland. After a minute, Vanessa's voice broke through the static: "Who is it?"

"Grace," I said. The buzzer rang and I went in. I took the elevator to the fourth floor. She stood behind the opened door of her apartment in a pink terry cloth bath robe, sipping from a cup, her hair uncombed.

I looked around the room, a small living room with a dining alcove at the far end, off the kitchen. "You got a new couch," I said. I walked over to the tufted black Naugahyde couch and sat down. "Good choice." I knew my father must have paid for it.

Scattered newspapers covered the glass coffee table. A brown and black striped sweater hung lopsided over the arm of a chair, a pair of jeans lay on the floor. I felt Vanessa's eyes on me as I looked around.

"What's up?" she asked, ignoring my reference to the couch.

"Nothing much," I said. "I was in your neighborhood. I thought maybe you wanted to do something. See a movie or something."

"Um . . . I don't know," she said. "I'm not dressed or anything."

"It's four in the afternoon."

"I'm capable of telling time, Grace. Did you come here to pass judgment on my habits?" she snapped.

Less than a minute had passed and things were already deteriorating. I needed to do better.

"Sorry," I said.

She leaned forward, gathering the newspapers and a few magazines into a neat pile. "So why don't you tell me why you're really here?" She wasn't looking at me. "I mean, I can't even remember the last time we went to the movies together." She picked up a brush and started stroking her hair.

I began slowly, trying not to provoke her. "Dad called me," I said. She held the hair brush in mid-air, waiting. "He's worried about you."

She tossed the brush onto the coffee table. It hit the glass and fell to the floor. "That's nice," she said, sarcastically, her lip curled with contempt. "What's the occasion?"

"Are you angry at Dad? Or just me?" I asked. I felt a hot flush on the back of my neck.

She got up and walked into her bedroom, returning minutes later in a pair of jeans and a sweatshirt, the University of Buffalo printed in large white letters across the front.

"Okay," she said, taking the seat across from me. "What's the agenda here?"

"I don't get it, Vanessa. Why are you so angry?"

She shrugged. "All I know, Grace, is it seems like you came to get a good look at the road kill. You're rubbernecking."

I bit my lip. We eyed each other suspiciously until, finally, I looked away.

Eventually I broke the silence. "Dad's worried that you aren't getting on with your life. He hoped you'd find a job and get past this Michael Wheatley mess."

Her face narrowed into a frown but she said nothing.

I began again. "Dad heard that Michael Wheatley took out an order of protection." I held my breath, not knowing how she'd react to this incriminating piece of news.

She reached over and picked up an issue of Glamour from the pile on the table and began flipping through the pages. "You seem to have forgotten I was acquitted. That means not guilty, Grace. It was unanimous."

"I'm not the enemy, Vanessa."

She stared at the magazine, ignoring me.

"It's not worth it," I went on. "It's only going to make things worse."

She flipped the magazine shut. "Yes. And here sits Princess Grace, the paragon of personal happiness. Any other advice you have for me?" She opened the magazine again and began reading.

I sat back in my chair and waited. Why was I even here?

Eventually she looked at me. "I know you think everything is my fault," she said. "Each and every one of those men made promises to me. Each and every one!"

She looked at me with disgust, her face taut. "And all of them broke those promises. They're all scum," her voice trailed off.

"I believe you," I said. "So . . . let go and move on. Pursuing Michael Wheatley won't get you anything but more trouble."

"Pursuing him!" She was nearly shouting. "Is that what you think? That I'm pursuing him?" She looked at me incredulously.

"What are you doing, Vanessa?"

"This is his payback. I'm giving him what he deserves." She sighed heavily, shaking her head.

"And what's in it for you?" I asked, leaning forward in the chair, studying her face. "What are you getting from it?"

She looked back at me, her eyes glazed. "I'm getting even. That's all. Even."

She opened the magazine again. A tear appeared at the corner of her eye and coursed a path down her cheek. She raised her left arm and brushed it away with her sleeve, her eyes still on the open magazine. She started chewing on her upper lip.

"Vanessa," I said softly, feeling a sudden pang of sympathy. "Let's go to a movie. **Eyes Wide Shut** is playing over on Main Street."

She let the magazine close. "Why?"

"Because we have to start somewhere."

We walked single file down the partially shoveled sidewalk. The frigid February air had formed a frozen crust on the snow, turned to splotchy black by dirt and traffic exhaust. Large garbage-filled plastic bags, awaiting pick-up, were piled high at the curb in front of each building. I looked at

Vanessa, walking ahead of me. How would all this end for her? It depressed me to think about it.

After the movie, we went to a nearby Chinese restaurant and sat at a small table facing each other. Watching her maneuver the chopsticks around a cashew nut, I tried to think of a safe topic when, suddenly, she blurted, "Grace, what did Dad say about me?" She kept her eyes on her food, but I could see her lower lip quivering.

"Just that he's worried. He wants you to find a job." I lowered my voice, hoping she wouldn't take offense.

"Did he say anything bad?" she asked, her jaw tightening. When she dropped her chopsticks onto the plate, I noticed her fingernails, bitten down to the flesh.

"He would never. You know that."

She got quiet again.

"Vanessa, why don't you talk to him? You know, about what you're doing. It seems like you want to. The two of you shouldn't need an intermediary."

"Butt out, Grace. It's none of your business."

Ignoring the bait, I changed the subject. "Do you know Mom lives only a few blocks from here?" I asked.

She shrugged and continued eating. I didn't try to fill the silence. We'd be done with dinner in a few minutes. I just needed to get through it.

But, surprisingly, it was Vanessa who spoke. "She called me."

"Who?" I asked.

"Mom."

"What did she say?"

"She wanted to meet for dinner. I told her not in this lifetime."

I tried to suppress a smile. I could hear her saying it.

"She disgusts me," she said, looking up at me. I sat back in my chair and watched her pick at her food, relieved she'd found some other target for her anger.

"I know you think I slept with Paul," she went on, her eyes meeting mine, challenging. Her right hand, holding the chopsticks, had started to shake.

Dumbfounded, I stared at her. After a few seconds, I heard my own voice, full of sarcasm. "Really. And how do you know that?"

"He told me."

I felt like I had been slapped. Under the table, I squeezed my hands together between my knees. "You mean . . . you talked to Paul after that day?"

She shrugged and started eating.

"Why did you bring this up?" I asked.

No response. She knew she had gotten to me, that she was in control again.

"I guess you don't care what I think of you," I said, my stomach churning.

I thought she might offer some protest, but she just kept eating, pushing the rice around her plate with the chopsticks. I wanted to lean across the table and yank them out of her hand.

Finally, looking squarely at me, she said, "Everything always works for you, Grace. Why do you get to have it so fucking easy? What'd you ever do to deserve it?"

I took a deep breath and shuddered. "I can't even stand to look at you. You've alienated everyone in your life and now me. No wonder you're alone. Someone would have to be insane to be with you."

My chair made an abrasive scraping noise as I pushed it back from the table. I dropped fifteen dollars next to her water glass, grabbed my jacket and walked out. A blast of frigid air hit my face. I took a step back into the doorway. Putting my jacket on, I spotted her through the window, her face now collapsed, her shoulders heaving with sobs. I stared at her through the glass pane until, finally, I pulled my zipper closed and ran most of the three blocks to the subway.

*　　*　　*

My father and I met for lunch two weeks later. We sat at our usual corner table in the Four Brothers Diner. I took small bites of my grilled cheese sandwich, waiting for the inevitable questions about Vanessa.

"Did you get to see Vanessa?" he asked, right on cue.

"I don't want to talk about Vanessa," I said, narrowing my eyes for emphasis.

Our eyes locked as I watched him close his mouth, stifling his response. "Please . . . don't ask me. Not any more."

He nodded slowly and cleared his throat. "Is there something else you'd like to talk about?" he asked.

I reached for my water glass. "Well, maybe . . . let's talk about you. Tell me why you became an engineer."

He smiled at me. "I was always puttering with things when I was a kid, you know, taking them apart—radios, toasters, whatever. I wanted to understand how the pieces fit together, how things worked mechanically. Then in high school, one of my teachers—Mr. Hammond, my chemistry teacher—he encouraged me to study engineering after he saw a weather station I designed.

"Why did you do it?" I asked.

"For a city-wide science contest."

"Did you win?" I asked.

"Third place." He started to laugh. "The prize was a yellow ribbon. Gram baked a cake for me. With lemon icing."

I smiled, remembering my grandmother's lemon cakes. Then impulsively, "How about Mom? How did the two of you end up together?"

He dunked a piece of bread into his soup. "You know, Grace . . . it was a long time ago," he said. "Things were very different then. Your mother and I met in our second year at Brooklyn College. We ended up in the same biology lab. Both of us had lost our lab partners for some reason—I don't remember now. Anyway, we became lab partners. She was so beautiful . . ." His voice trailed. "And in those days, quick to laugh. I was very taken with her." A reluctant smile flickered across his face.

I tried to imagine my mother . . . young, laughing, but I couldn't conjure up the image. It wasn't the Margaret Strickland I remembered.

"I left college to get a job after my third year. My father had gotten sick and my family needed the money. I'm sure I've told you this before."

"I know you had to leave school, but I've never really understood why you and Mom ended up together. I mean . . . the two of you . . . you're so . . ."

"It was another time, Grace. Everything about it was different. I was working, going to school at night. Over night I became responsible for my whole family. Your mother was the single bright spot in my life."

I watched my father intently as he spoke. The idea of my mother as a bright spot was beyond my imagining. "So what changed?" I asked.

"When we got married, she went to work so I could finish my degree. At night there was the house work, the laundry. She became very serious."

"And then when George died . . ." he let his spoon drop on the table. "Well that changed everything." His voice fell to a near whisper.

"I thought things would get better when Vanessa was born but . . . they got worse. It seemed like everything I did made your mother angry. After awhile, well . . . there just wasn't anything left."

I could see the weariness in his face, the fatigue around his eyes. I stared at him, remembering the times he had slept on the couch, the blustering arguments, the angry silences.

He picked up his napkin and blotted his forehead. "Our marriage turned into a nightmare. For both of us."

He folded the napkin and put it on his lap. "I still don't understand how that happened, how we went from A to Z," his voice suddenly hoarse. He cleared his throat. "Our marriage was over when we buried George. We just didn't know it then."

"I'm sorry, Dad," I whispered, forcing the words past the ache in my throat.

I looked down at my half-eaten sandwich. I didn't know what else to say. I had blamed my father for things he did, for things he didn't do. For Vanessa, for Valerie. I had judged him without knowing, without understanding what it must have felt like for him to imagine a future trapped, without hope.

*   *   *

Dreams about my mother intruded on my sleep.

I was meeting her at a luncheon where she was to receive an award. I lost the address and never found the building.

My mother and I were walking together on the street. She tripped and fell on a break in the cement. I kept going, pretending not to hear her calling to me for help.

I hadn't seen my mother since our last disastrous dinner almost five months earlier. We had spoken, awkwardly, on the phone but sheer dread trumped any sense of duty for me. Now, however, I wanted to hear her side of the story.

We met at Guilio's, a small Italian restaurant around the corner from her office. I resisted going to her apartment, filled as it was with reminders of Wentworth Street—the sterling tea service which rattled every time she slammed a door, the mahogany dining room breakfront into which she had thoughtlessly tossed a year's worth of Erin's letters.

She was already seated when I arrived. I forced myself to smile and, meekly, she smiled back, fiddling nervously with her napkin, folding it, refolding it, before placing it carefully on the red and white gingham tablecloth. A plate of antipasto sat in front of her, untouched.

"I'm glad you called, Grace. I've been . . . hoping we could get together."

"How've you been?" I asked.

"Fine, mostly." She ran her finger nail over the stem of her wine glass. "I've been . . . uh . . . sort of preoccupied with some of the things you said last time." She started to cough, then fumbled through her purse, pulling out a cough drop.

"I want you to know I called Vanessa," she said, looking squarely at me for the first time. "I asked her to have dinner with me, but she said no." She looked around the restaurant, then back at me. "I'm going to try again . . . soon."

I knew she wouldn't but I let the comment pass. "What exactly happened between you and Vanessa?" I asked.

"Well, I called . . .

"No, not that," I interrupted. "I mean, from the beginning, when she was a child."

She sighed heavily and sat back in her chair. "God, Grace, I don't know. It's too hard for me to go back through all of that. Those years . . . they were so painful."

An image flashed through my head, a younger version of my mother, raising her hand to slap Vanessa. "I'm asking you because it's important to me. I need to know," I added for emphasis.

"What is it, Grace? What exactly do you want to know?" Wispy strands of gray hair fell over her ear and onto her face. She pushed them back with her fingers. Long, slender fingers. I looked down at my own, short and stubby. A stranger passing us would not imagine we were related.

"For one thing, why did you hate Vanessa?"

My bluntness must have startled her. Wide-eyed, she looked at me, then down at her lap, her hand trembling as she reached for her glass of wine.

"It wasn't Vanessa really," her voice barely above a whisper, her eyes avoiding mine. She didn't go on.

"Well . . . then what was it?" I would hammer it out of her if I had to.

A minute or two passed before she began again, clutching onto her wine glass as if it were holding her steady. "When George was killed, I felt . . . I don't know . . . betrayed, I guess. I thought I had suffered enough." She started to cough and waved to the waiter to bring a glass of water.

"Please don't stop," I said, urging her on.

She tried to smile. "When I met your father, I felt like my luck had finally changed. He made me laugh and he was a kind good man. I loved that in him and talked myself into marrying him. I knew he would be a good husband and father. He wouldn't drink away his paycheck. He was always so responsible."

"So what went wrong?" I asked, ignoring the implication that, in marrying my father, she had settled.

A look of surprise spread across her face as if she thought I should've known.

"What went wrong," she said, with a raw edge of exasperation, "was that George died." She looked away, pressing the heel of her hand against her forehead. It had been almost 40 years, yet the pain in that simple gesture grabbed at me.

She hesitated before continuing. "I would've been there on that driveway with him, but your father and I were arguing about something stupid. Something totally meaningless." She blew her nose again. "Believe me, Grace, I've blamed myself too."

"But I don't understand what all this has to do with Vanessa."

"It's not easy . . . I don't know . . ." She looked around the room again, then back at me. "Tell me why we need to go over all of this."

"It's my family history. Don't you think I'm entitled to know it?"

She sighed heavily. "I was angry at your father because he recovered so quickly. From George's death, I mean. I felt the pain, the awful emptiness every single day, but he moved on. Without a problem, it seemed to me. He brought home all these presents for Vanessa, three, four times a week. It was . . . I don't know . . . it was almost like Vanessa's birth erased George's death for him."

She sat back in her chair, staring off somewhere beyond me, her eyes shiny and wet. She looked fragile with her ivory silk blouse giving softness to her face, nothing like the villainous images I'd hoarded in my memory. She was still an unusually pretty woman. She and Vanessa both . . . connected by their looks and their contempt for each other.

I waited for her to go on, to give me an explanation that made sense to me.

Her voice dropped and I had to strain to hear her. "I can't make it right by explaining it. If I've learned anything in my training, it's that people need to find a way to forgive themselves. And . . . if they're lucky, others will forgive them too."

She looked straight at me for only a moment. I hadn't forgiven her—she knew this without asking. And, it occurred to me later, she forgave herself by making my father the villain.

"It happened and I couldn't control it. Now it's just easier for me to start over with Herb's grandchildren than it is to fix things with Vanessa. She doesn't want to hear anything from me." Her eyes narrowed on mine. "And I know how that feels," she said, gritting her teeth, "because I felt the same way about my own mother who failed me and my brothers in every conceivable way. Worse than anything you think I'm guilty of."

"So that's your explanation? That you weren't as bad as your mother?"

"Grace, what happened was more than thirty-five years ago, and I wasn't the only one there." Her voice rose and I could see her jaw tensing, tightening like a stretched rubber band. Her eyes suddenly focused on mine, laser-like. "He chose Vanessa over me. He left me mired in my grief."

I pressed my back into the cushioned frame of the chair and looked across the table at her. She had been mean and self-absorbed, at times even worse. Had I expected her to admit she'd been a rotten mother? I'm not sure, but I had to let it go now. It wasn't going to get any better than this.

8/8/00

Hi Erin,

New developments on the Strickland front over the past several months. Vanessa's had a few questionable accidents. First she broke her arm when she fell off a ladder while changing a light bulb in her kitchen. Several weeks after that, she took an "accidental" overdose of tranquilizers. In a stupor, she called my father, who took her to the hospital. Then a few weeks ago she was hit by a car. She wasn't seriously injured but did get banged up and two of her ribs were broken. The lawyer my father hired told him a witness said Vanessa seemed to walk deliberately in front of the car. Now my father is taking care of everything, paying her bills, etc. I haven't gone to see her yet—I'm trying to decide what to do. Part of me thinks she's just being manipulative, but I am worried that she'll really hurt herself. What if she kills herself? She could do it just to spite us. My father would be devastated.

I need advice.

love grace

8/21/00

Hi,

Not good news about Vanessa. I wish I knew what to tell you.

I'm struggling with my own family drama. We heard from father's sister that he's been diagnosed with lymphoma and is getting treatments in the prison hospital. I was really thrown by this news and am having trouble sleeping. I don't want to know anything about him. I took me years to stop thinking about him every day and now here I am again. I hardly think of anything else.

Sorry you caught me in such a foul mood.

E

Fourteen months later, Erin and I stood side by side in a Queens cemetery, watching a simple pine coffin as Miss Zrinsky's body was lowered into the ground. I felt a raw pain in the back of my throat and clutched Erin's arm.

At the end of the service, an elderly woman, taller and heavier than Miss Zrinsky, walked over and extended her hand to Erin. "I see the red hair and know you are Erin," she said softly. She turned to me. "And you must be Grace," she continued. "Always, Hannah speaks often about you. She vould be happy to know you are here."

"Frieda?" asked Erin.

"Yes. I am Frieda. Please valk now with me and meet Albert—Hannah's brother, Albert," she said. She led us around the open grave to a section of folding chairs where Albert was seated. He resembled Miss Zrinsky, small in stature, deep lines chiseled into his round face. His left hand, covering the right, trembled with what I surmised was Parkinson's.

"Albert," said Frieda, gently touching his shoulder. "This is Hannah's Grace and Erin."

Red-eyed, he squinted, his face turned upward toward us. A middle-aged woman in her 50's helped him to his feet. He leaned on a cane for support.

"Thank you for coming," he said. "I am happy to meet you. You girls . . . I see you are not any longer girls . . . so often Hannah talked about you." He took a handkerchief from his pocket and wiped his eyes. A cough shook his body.

"Excuse me," he whispered. "I vant you should meet Rose, my vife Rose," he said, reaching behind to the woman seated next to him. "And my daughter Molly," he continued, turning to the woman who had helped him to his feet. They smiled at us. Albert began coughing again and Molly eased him back into his chair. With his hand shaking, he patted the handkerchief against his mouth.

Again Frieda stepped forward. "We sit shiva now for Hannah. My family vent back to the house to prepare. I hope you can join us. Everyone will vant to meet you, we hear so much about you."

Erin and I glanced at each other. "Of course we'll go," she said.

"This is a difficult time now for us," Frieda said, as we walked to my father's car which I had borrowed for the day. "My husband died a few years ago . . . and now Hannah." She dabbed at her eyes with a lace handkerchief. "Hannah was the closest person to me. I am grateful we had many years together. Others were not as fortunate."

Erin and I followed Frieda's car, as she led the way to her house, a modest split-level in East Meadow, Long Island. There we met her sons and their wives, their children, their grandchildren. Their family alone filled the small house. It was as Miss Zrinsky had once said, out of ashes they had made a new family.

Photographs of Miss Zrinsky, taken with other family members, were displayed on the fireplace mantle and tables throughout the house. Smiling, pushing a baby carriage, standing arm-in-arm with a girl in a blue cap and gown, lighting candles in a menorah. Fragments of Miss Zrinsky's life, no longer beyond our reach.

More people arrived, Albert and his family, a few library employees and others we didn't know. Some brought food. A rabbi appeared and said prayers in Hebrew. After people began talking quietly, Frieda came over and sat with us. "Please have something to eat," she said. "Whenever you are ready to leave, Molly vill show you the way back."

"Frieda," I began. "I want you to know that Erin and I . . . we were deeply moved by the story Miss Zrinsky told us . . . about your escape from Poland. I've thought of it so many times."

Frieda sighed, a deep sigh. "Hannah vas the strongest one. She kept us going."

"She said the same thing about you," Erin interjected.

Frieda shook her head. "The truth is . . . Hannah held us all the time together. When Aleksander—do you know about the man who picked us up in his vagon?" she asked.

"Yes," said Erin. "That was where you first met. Under the blanket in the wagon."

"Yes, it vas." Frieda, caught up in the memory, was slow to respond. "Aleksander took us to the train." Frieda looked down at her hands. She stayed quiet for a minute or so.

"Molly vas all the time afraid," Frieda continued. "She vanted to stay, to look for Albert and their parents. She vas clinging to Aleksander, crying. In the end, Hannah half carried Molly onto the train."

"Molly cried a long time," Frieda continued, her own eyes now wet with tears. "Until she fell asleep. Only then did Hannah cry. It vas very hard on her."

Frieda pulled a handkerchief from her pocket and wiped her eyes. Erin and I looked at each other, not knowing what to say.

"Then when Molly got sick," Frieda spoke quietly, "Hannah hid her in our room. She knew the others in the rooming house vould make us leave because everyone was afraid of catching the typhoid. For Hannah, Molly always came first."

Just as Frieda stopped talking and raised the handkerchief to her mouth, Erin reached out to touch her arm. As I watched Frieda struggle to regain her composure, I felt tears on my own face.

"Hannah never had her own family. When ve were young, she vas engaged to be married. Saul Fine . . . she met him in the Queens College. I vas also then engaged to my husband. Ve had such plans, to raise our children together. But Saul got polio. He vas paralyzed down from the neck and put in the iron lung. He died in a few months."

Erin and I looked at each other, stunned by this new revelation. So this was why she never married! Had she never gotten over it? I shook my head and shivered. I didn't want to hear anymore. I couldn't stand knowing another awful thing Miss Zrinsky had lived through.

Ted

A year after Miss Zrinsky's funeral, I moved to Phoenix. Even after four years, those two events remained elementally linked for me because, if not for her, I might not have gone through with the move.

When I received the job offer to oversee recruitment in American Express's Phoenix office, my reaction was decidedly negative. Phoenix? Shit. What would I do there? I hate golf . . . I get rashes from the sun . . . I don't know anybody . . . I'd be a million miles from my family.

I actually tried to make a list of pros and cons but couldn't dredge up a single pro. Yet the pull to move nagged at me, and I couldn't seem to foreclose on it with any finality. Thoughts about my career, stagnant for some time, finally prodded me out of inertia. Okay, I said to myself, I'll look for another job. In New York.

Still, I ruminated, mentally hacking away at my list of cons. I knew the Phoenix job would be a substantial promotion, a pro that should've made it to my list. And the cons . . . what did they really amount to? I could wear sunscreen. Eventually I'd meet people. And the distance from my family? Not hard to imagine an upside to that.

I kept thinking of Miss Zrinsky, how she had traveled from Poland to New York at half my age, and despite losing her family and everything else, she had figured out a way to start over. She'd been my role model since I was twelve years old, a steadfast and remarkable presence throughout my adolescence. Would she have told me to move?

And Erin. Uprooted from her home and tossed around among random relatives, also at half my age.

I crumpled my list of cons and, six weeks later, got off the plane at the Phoenix airport. At the gate, a rush of anxiety sent my heart beating into the stratosphere, and I stopped walking to take in slow deep breaths, inhale one-two-three, exhale one-two-three, over and over until, finally, my attention focused on a pair of unidentifiable hands holding a cardboard "STRICKLAND" sign. Unidentifiable, that is, until I got close enough to see the red hair ducking behind the cardboard.

I grabbed the sign from Erin and pulled her close. Blinking back tears, I said, "Here you are, helping me again."

She squeezed my arm, laughing, pulling me toward the baggage claim area.

"Erin, what are you doing in Phoenix?"

"Surprising you. I still remember what it's like to get off a plane alone in a strange city."

"I'm so glad you're here," I whispered. "I feel like I'm in a foreign country."

"Leaving New York must've traumatized you."

"It was hard. I haven't really processed it yet since I've been distracted by all the farewell events. Last week, a bunch of friends took me out for dinner, and my co-workers surprised me with a party. Saturday afternoon, I saw Andrea Jaeger for a few hours. I told you she got divorced, then her mother died. She looked ashen when I got up to leave. I felt so bad for her . . . she reminded me of myself when you left. One more abandonment was not what she needed."

"What about your family? Did you see Vanessa?"

"No. Just my parents. Separately of course. I left a phone message for Vanessa to meet my father and me for dinner, but she didn't show up. Truthfully, I only did it so I wouldn't feel guilty about slipping away without saying good-bye. But it's all on her now. I'm just going to focus on what I need to do for myself."

We dragged my suitcases over to a nearby taxi stand. "Let's drop your stuff at the hotel. Then we can explore downtown Phoenix," said Erin.

"Tell me about you," I said. "Any more news about your father?"

She shook her head. "My sister Kate got married. We all flew to Kansas City for the wedding. I brought pictures to show you. All my brothers and sisters and nobody's smiling. Getting together upsets us all. We don't talk about my father but just being together sparks the memories . . . and the shame. We look at each other and see my father. It's like there's no way to move on."

*   *   *

I was fine until two days later when Erin went back to Omaha, and I was on my own, left to find my solitary way through the sun-filled rainless maze. The strangeness of the city overwhelmed me, the unfamiliar streets, the weird low Pueblo-style buildings and palm trees, the endless unshaded heat. I quickly saw that survival meant air-conditioning and long walks down Lexington Avenue, or any avenue, were not in my future.

I picked up a rental car from Avis and spent the next half-hour driving around haplessly just to find a supermarket. There were maps in the glove compartment and I kept pulling over to get my bearings, but I began to wonder if I ever had bearings.

At the end of the first week, I pulled into a gas station only to discover that people are expected to pump their own gas. Someday it is possible

I will laugh at the memory of myself standing outside a blue Toyota Corolla, credit card in hand and eyes welling with frustrated tears. The next morning at 7:00, I was back at Avis learning how to remove the gas cap which, of course, did not simply twist off but had to be jiggled in some counter-intuitive way.

I met the eight people on my staff the first morning on the job, immediately following the gas cap tutorial at Avis. Two of the men, both older than me, had been contenders for my job. Walter Witson, the more aggressive one, would challenge me in every staff meeting with extraneous facts and details gathered over his many years in the department. He would undermine my decisions so regularly that simply anticipating his opposition kept me off balance. It unsettled me the way he watched me, his weasel eyes following me as I went to the conference room, the restroom, the copy machine, wherever. At the end of my second week, I left the office one morning for a meeting and, getting into my car, I saw him looking at me, sneering from a second-story office window. He was getting to me.

Then there was Roger, a short, rotund man who, despite the intense Arizona sun, had a pallor close to porcelain, as if he'd been swallowed whole by some virus. Months passed before I realized that his stoop-shouldered fawner act camouflaged his real intent to sabotage me. He made sure I had access to reports with inherently false information, twice leading me to reverse long-standing policies only to be embarrassed later by the fallout. I wasn't doing as well as I had expected and a steady gnawing dread about my future there unnerved me.

Settling in to my newly-sublet townhouse was equally daunting. Each night after work, I stopped to get take-out from Burrito Mania and, sitting on a chair next to the stacked cartons in the kitchen, I would eat my dinner. I still cringe at the memory but it was better than eating alone in a restaurant filled with people who weren't alone.

Then I'd start unpacking boxes hoping to fill enough space to soften the echo that bounced off the walls whenever I talked on the phone. I taped black plastic garbage bags over my bedroom window to shut out the morning sun. One of the spare bedrooms became a makeshift office, with an aluminum folding table serving as a desk for the computer, my books stacked on the floor against the wall. Some of the loneliest nights of my life were spent in that room with me at the computer, struggling to stay focused on reports I'd brought home from work, distracted again and again by the headlights of passing cars streaming through the windows and exposing me, as I imagined, to the view of everyone on the block.

The myriad details involved in putting a household together overwhelmed me, and I thought longingly of my studio apartment in New York, a manageable 300 square feet. My father had given me his cast-off furniture and, one Saturday afternoon, had brought his drill and screwdriver over to install the window shades. I couldn't imagine why I'd rented a three-bedroom townhouse. I never managed to get comfortable there, rattling around room after empty room, squinting at the bare walls begging to be filled. I ached with a growing sense of isolation and doubted myself on the job. Moving had been a disastrous mistake.

*   *   *

I met my first friend in the home decorating department of a neighborhood hardware store. Sitting at a table next to the vertical blind display, she was flipping through pages of an oversized wallpaper book. "Shit," she muttered, winding one of her jet black braids around her index finger.

Looking over at her, I laughed.

"Sorry," she said, smiling. "I'm so sick of this."

"I'm right there myself." I collapsed into a chair opposite her. "I'll help you with your wallpaper if you pick out my window coverings."

"You have a deal." She extended her hand. "My name's Kathryn." She smiled, revealing a gap between her two front teeth, the only visible imperfection I could see. She had a beautiful face and a complexion so wholesome it reminded me of those television milk commercials.

"Mine's Grace." As we shook hands, I noticed the large turquoise ring on her right hand. An authentic Westerner, I thought to myself. "Are you from Phoenix?" I asked.

"I moved here about eight months ago, from Albuquerque. How about you?"

"I've been here two months. Too long to be without window shades," I said. "Why did you move?"

"For a job. I'm the director of an employees' assistance program for one of the big hotel chains."

"I could use some employees' assistance," I said, laughing. "But I'll wait 'til I know you better."

"Why wait? I'm dying to be rescued from these wallpaper books." Her dark brown eyes radiated warmth.

Not needing further encouragement, I plunged into complaints about Walter and Roger and the feeling I had of drowning in my own mistakes.

"A couple of years ago, I read a book about managing personalities. I can't think of the author's name at the moment, but he presents a lot of fairly typical scenarios that you might find helpful. I can email his name to you."

"Thanks," I said, pulling a business card from my wallet.

The following Saturday we met at the Heard Museum to see an exhibit on Native American crafts. I stood in the shadow cast by a UPS truck waiting for Kathryn's black braids to appear, but she bounded around the corner with her hair in a ponytail hanging loosely at her neck. When I walked over to greet her, I felt her height above me and, for a brief moment, thought of Vanessa, always those enviable few inches taller.

*   *   *

I hadn't seen my mother's brother Will in almost twenty years but, since I was headed to Chicago for a conference and knew he lived there, I looked up his phone number on the internet. I really wanted to hear his version of my messed-up family's history.

We arranged to meet at my hotel. When I got off the elevator, I saw him sitting in the lobby, drumming his fingers against his thigh. His hair had thinned considerably, but his face was instantly recognizable. I took a deep breath and walked over to him.

"Grace!" He stood up slowly and stared at me.

Awkwardly, we embraced and walked into the hotel restaurant, both of us stumbling through stiff greetings and small talk. In my anticipation, I thought we'd have an instantaneous connection, but a clumsy silence hung in the air.

"You look so much like my mother," I said, finally, eyeing him from across the table. "I might have recognized you even if I hadn't known you'd be here."

"Tell me about your mother. How is she?" The skin around his mouth tightened, strained with a familiar look of tension. I wondered what he expected from our meeting.

"She's doing well. She's the director of a community counseling agency that provides services to the schools and courts. Did you know she got a degree in social work?"

He shook his head.

"She's still involved with the bereavement center and has been on their board of directors for a bunch of years now. When did you speak to her last?"

He shrugged and took off his glasses, putting them on the table next to his napkin. "Honestly, Grace, I lost track, I'm sorry to say." The age lines in his forehead deepened as he spoke. "It's my biggest regret . . . still."

"Do you know about the trial?"

His eyes widened and he leaned toward me in his chair. "What trial?"

"Vanessa," I said, watching the shock flood his face. "She stalked some man and tried to blackmail him."

"What happened to her?"

"She was acquitted, but it's been a few years and she's still kind of at loose ends."

"My god, I had no idea." He put his glasses back on and looked at me. "How'd your mother hold up during the trial?"

"She wasn't there," I said quietly.

His eyes glazed as he slowly shook his head.

"It's been a mess . . . especially between my mother and Vanessa. Since we were kids."

He nodded sadly, knowingly.

"My mother was pretty mean to Vanessa. They fought constantly."

"How was she to you?" he asked.

"Not so good, but better to me than Vanessa. She was angry a lot, she'd give us the silent treatment for days at a time. I was . . . well . . . afraid of her."

He took off his glasses again and rubbed his eyes with a napkin.

"I'm sorry, Uncle Will. I guess I dove in without thinking. I shouldn't have said any of this."

"I'm glad you're telling me," he cut in. "I've wondered about so many of these things over the years." His eyes were fixed on mine. "What about your father?"

"My father left. One night everything exploded in one gigantic ugly episode. I was in high school then, Vanessa was in college. After that, it was just my mother and me, until I left for college."

"Grace, I'm sorry." He reached over, touching my arm. "I know I abandoned you. Your mother and I . . . our relationship deteriorated beyond . . . I didn't know how to fix it."

"What happened?" I asked.

He sighed heavily and picked up his water glass. "We got into an argument during a phone conversation. By that time, things had been tense for at least a year. She said I betrayed her, that I always took your father's side. She hung up on me. I called her back about a week later, but she wouldn't talk to me. Over a period of time, I wrote her a few letters but she never answered them. I knew she could carry a grudge forever."

He stopped talking and raked his fingers through his hair. "I should've done better but it frustrated me no end to watch her. I thought she was ruining her life. It seemed the only thing she could give herself to was grieving over George. I knew she expected me to be more sympathetic because we'd had a pretty bad time as kids . . . with our own parents. I didn't react the way she'd wanted me to."

We sat for awhile without speaking. Finally, he cleared his throat and said, "Grace, does your mother know about our brother Chris?"

The name startled me. "No. I mean, I don't think so. She never mentioned it."

"About ten or twelve years ago, there was a small article in the business section of a local paper about a promotion I'd gotten at Prudential. Some guy who'd been in Chris' platoon in Viet Nam saw it and got in touch with me. He told me that after the war Chris went back to Viet Nam to look for a woman he had fallen in love with. Turns out he never found her but he stayed there and eventually married someone else. He died about two years later when a fishing boat he was working on capsized during a storm.

"I wrote to Margaret to tell her but never heard back from her. I should've called then. I don't even know if she got the letter." He stared at his plate, shaking his head.

I watched his face, shrouded, pained. I wanted to say—why don't you just put it all aside and call her? But I didn't. I knew what I'd say if someone asked me the same question about Vanessa.

*   *   *

"So, how was Chicago?" Kathryn and I had planted ourselves on the bench outside Jamba Juice a few days after I got back.

"Surprisingly good. I met some new people who could be good networking contacts. And I took a workshop on strategies for dealing with difficult employees."

"Does that mean Walter with the eyes isn't giving you a break? I'm curious to hear what you learned."

"It boils down to two choices. I can pretend he doesn't exist—as long as I can pull it off convincingly. Or I can confront him."

"Which one appeals to you?"

"Neither," I said, laughing. "I'm hoping you'll tell me what you'd do."

"Did you get to see your uncle?" She jabbed at her banana smoothie with a straw.

"Yeah, I did. We dug up some old family skeletons." I hesitated, unsure of how much I wanted to say.

Kathryn looked up at me. "It sounds intriguing."

"Seeing him got me to thinking about my sister. I mean, my uncle and my mother haven't spoken in maybe twenty years, and I've started to realize that Vanessa and I are travelling down that same road."

"Do you want to tell me what happened between you?"

I groaned. "A lifetime of slings and arrows."

"Do you think you'll get in touch with her?"

I shrugged listlessly.

"What's stopping you? It seems like you're considering it."

I sighed. "It never works. It just makes things worse because then I'm left with the aftermath, choking on my anger for weeks, or longer even. I swear, sometimes in the thick of it, I feel positively contaminated . . . like poison is shooting through my bloodstream. I walk around muttering to myself, having imaginary conversations with Vanessa, trying to unload all the things I should've said. I dread going through it again. But enough about me. We've never talked about your family."

Hesitating, Kathryn speared a piece of banana with her straw and when she glanced over at me, I could see a tinge of sadness in her eyes. "It's just me and my mother. I used to tell people that my father died but the truth is he just left us. When I was four. After it happened, my mom and I lived in our car for almost a year. We got food from the church and washed ourselves in public restrooms. Somehow my mother pulled us out of that abyss. Everything I know about personal resolve and dignity, I learned from her."

"Where is she now?"

"In Albuquerque. She owns a jewelry business," said Kathryn, holding up the turquoise ring I had noticed the day we met. "She makes most of it herself."

"Do you see her often?"

"Once every month or two, but we talk almost every day. Next time she comes to Phoenix, I'll invite you over for a barbeque. But Grace, I just wanted to get back to you and your sister for a minute. When you said you dreaded going through the whole negative cycle with her again, it struck me that you are going through it, whether you're talking to her or not."

"I don't get what you mean."

"Don't you see all the energy you're consuming just to keep your distance? It must be exhausting."

*   *   *

Thoughts of Vanessa took over, distracting me at work and keeping me awake at night. I hadn't seen her since our dinner at the Chinese restaurant when she'd confirmed all my suspicions about her relationship with Paul. She must've really hated me, the way she'd flung it in my face, the whole time sitting there gawking at my reaction. Well, she wasn't alone. I hated her too.

But Kathryn's point had sunk in. Vanessa was still anchored in the middle of my life, and the intervening years had not changed that single immutable fact. I had not escaped her by avoiding her. Still, I did nothing, letting the weeks become months.

*   *   *

I met Ted on a Friday. I'd been looking forward to unwinding in the jaccuzzi after a particularly chaotic week, but when I got home, my voicemail light flashed with a message from Kathryn. A college friend was having a party. She'd pick me up at 8 pm.

As we walked in, I saw a group of men flocked together in a corner watching a televised basketball game. I noticed him immediately because he wasn't yelling at the TV like the others. Later, Kathryn and I were in the kitchen talking when he came in.

"Ted!" Kathryn's face broke into a smile. "What are you doing here? I thought you lived in San Diego."

His gaze inched across my face before he turned to her. "I moved here a few months ago for a job in the legal department at Bank of America. How about you?"

"I've been here nearly a year, working for Marriott," Kathryn said. "Let me introduce you to my friend, Grace. Grace, this is Ted Marshall. Ted and I lived on the same floor in a dorm at the University of Arizona."

His smile drew me in, his eyes again lingering on my face.

"I see you're a basketball fan," I said, smiling back at him.

"I am but unfortunately basketball season is almost over."

"So what happens then?" I asked, tilting my head to the side, flirtatiously.

"Baseball season." He grinned broadly and my gaze rested on his enviable dimples. "Quickly followed by football season."

"What? No tennis or golf?"

"I find some time for tennis and golf but they're not top priority," he said, laughing.

*   *   *

On our first date, three nights later, we met for dinner at an outdoor cafe. In the distance, a lush green golf course filled the horizon.

"Is there a message here?" I said, smiling at him.

"Only subliminally." The light sparkled in his eyes, locked together with mine.

"You know, Phoenix has four professional sports teams," he said, teasingly.

"And an opera," I quipped. "How are you with equal time?"

"Are you an opera fan? Say no, please." Still smiling, he covered my hand with his.

"Actually, the truth is I'm not. But I do love theatre. And movies most of all."

"We'll see what we can work out." When his hand squeezed mine, adrenaline shot through my body.

"So . . . do you excel at all these sports?"

"You've seen through my façade already. I defaulted to being a sports fan as a defensive strategy. I have three very athletic brothers and it seems they got all the good genes. My oldest brother Bruce tried to help me, but even with hours of practice in the back yard, I never found my groove as a competitive athlete. But I do excel at spectating."

"Were you disappointed?" I asked, leaning toward him, breathing in the scent from his after-shave.

"I got over it," he said quietly. "But my father didn't."

*   *   *

He called the next afternoon. "I hope you're free tomorrow night because I had to arm wrestle one of my cohorts for two tickets to Blood Brothers at the Phoenix Theatre."

I pressed the phone against my ear. "I'd love to go. I hope you won't be missing a basketball game."

He laughed. "I'm trying to recreate my image in your eyes."

"It's working. I'm already seeing the new you. And I even liked the old you."

"Great. So I'm off to a good start?" I could hear the smile in his voice. My hand, gripping the phone, tensed with excitement.

"Last night was great . . . really," I whispered.

"Yeah, for me too," he said.

*   *   *

We saw each other four nights that first week. On the weekend, he came over with his toolbox and tightened every loose nut and bolt, cleared a clogged showerhead, replaced a broken light switch and hung my pictures.

"You desperately need a handyman." His dimpled face grinned down at me from the ladder.

"I think I've found one," I said, beaming up at him, my body taut with desire.

He put the screwdriver in his back pocket, stepped off the ladder and lifted me off the ground. As I buried my face in his shoulder, he whispered, "You have. You have found one."

He was a cold glass of water on a blistering day, and I gulped him in. His presence grounded me, filling me with a euphoria I had not imagined possible. I pulsed with exuberant energy.

Kathryn and I met at a movie a few weeks later. Afterwards we sat at our usual bench outside Jamba Juice.

"So, I'm dying to know. There's not been a single juicy detail in any of your emails."

"I'm . . . it's . . . oh god, I can't even find the words. I keep thinking of a line from an Elizabeth Barrett Browning poem about 'everyday's most quiet need'—I don't remember the rest of it. I can visualize a tiny space in my core that no one before has ever touched."

"Your most quiet need. God, I'm jealous."

"It probably sounds corny," I said.

"It sounds great. But . . . I want to say . . . be careful. It's just the beginning."

"I know. Every once in awhile I start hyperventilating. Last night I dreamt I was supposed to meet him but I couldn't find my car. I ran around the neighborhood in a frenzy looking for the car, waking up agitated and out-of-breath. Afraid that all my long-buried insecurities might suffocate me."

"I know the feeling. I've always thought of it as the dark side of sheer bliss." Kathryn leaned over and squeezed my shoulder. "All those old fears of abandonment we try to squelch get to us when we're vulnerable."

"I don't want to be vulnerable," I whispered, covering my face with my hands. "I want this to go on forever."

*   *   *

Ted and I took off for a weekend in Sedona. Despite the stack of vacation brochures on the back seat of his car, we spent most of Saturday morning in our room at the Bed & Breakfast. I floated in space, my body weightless and electrified. We made love voraciously, again and again, until the need for food forced us out. After lunch, we walked unhurriedly along a mountain road to the Chapel of the Holy Cross, his arm around my back, his hand clutching my waist. I leaned against him, savoring his scent and the quiet gentleness in his voice. At dusk, we rented a canoe and paddled for two hours on the river, the quiet calm interrupted only by the clamor of honking geese and our laughter.

After the long weekend, we drove back to Phoenix and our separate homes. I alternated between profound elation and a gradual accumulating apprehension. Memories of past betrayals haunted me. In a dream, I saw Paul and Simone Agnelli, from Vanessa's trial, pushing a shopping cart together down the aisle at Food City.

I knew Ted could ditch me for an old girlfriend or get scared and disappear. I did my best to squelch these fears but I caved into them more often than I wanted to admit. A few times I stooped to checking the outgoing calls on his cell phone and once even looked at his email. I knew anything was possible. I had known him only five weeks.

But he didn't disappear. After three months, we moved many of my clothes into his two-bedroom condo though I still had several months left on my townhouse sublet. We flew to the San Juan Islands for five days and booked a pre-Christmas trip to Hawaii. We began imagining a future together, and I nestled into a sense of safety I had never known before.

1/27/07

Hi Erin,

I'm finally downloading the pictures we took last weekend. Tracey reminds me so much of you—the way she shakes her head to fluff out her hair and chews on her bottom lip. And freckles everywhere, even on her eyelids and lips—just like you. I'll thank you forever for bringing her here. For once, I was happy to have rented the townhouse so you could have your own rooms.

I'm so glad Ted got to meet you—and vice versa of course. It would've been perfect if Calvin could have been here. Too bad he has to work weekends.

My father's been nudging me to visit for a couple of months, so I've finally decided to go next week. Since it will be my first trip back, I've told Ted I need to go alone. It's a little awkward—I've met his whole family but, as you know, it's complicated enough without him there. I'm committed to avoiding unnecessary drama.

Things are just so good between us . . . . I just never really imagined . . .

much love,

2/1/07

Hi Grace,

Tracey's still talking about you. She immediately told Calvin the story about my getting lost in the Museum of Natural History on our 5th grade class trip and you finding me close to tears, wandering around the Hall of African Mammals.

I'm amazed you still have the friendship ring with my name inscribed. When did we get those? 7th grade? I haven't seen mine since I left New York. Now Tracey and her friend Janine are talking about getting rings.

It was great meeting Ted. I loved watching him watch you. He looks at you like you're the only person in the room. When you told me about the conference you spoke at, he just beamed with pride. You've picked a winner!

Good luck in NY.

E

I really didn't want to see Vanessa but I forced myself to call her the night before my flight to New York.

"Hey, it's Vanessa. Leave a number at the beep." Having expected a lethargic monotone on the voice message, I was surprised to hear some energy in her voice.

"Hi Vanessa, it's me. I'm coming into New York for a few days and I . . . um . . . was hoping we could talk. I'll give you a call when I get to Lila's."

But when the time came, I put off the call and instead made plans to have lunch with my mother. We met at Sarabeth's on Madison Avenue, embracing awkwardly on the sidewalk in front of the restaurant. Once at the table, she rattled on about the Bereavement Center and Herb, her nervous energy triggering a slow pounding in my head until I wanted to scream at her to stop. I might as well have been chained to the chair. The barely-masked welter of tension and the tedium of her meaningless chatter exhausted me. How long did we have to maintain this pretense of caring about each other?

In an hour-and-a-half together, she asked me exactly two questions. How was my job and how was my apartment. I said it's a townhouse, not an apartment. Oh, she said. I was tempted to say—I guess you didn't look at the pictures I sent you, but I just let it go. Who even cared anymore.

I had planned to tell her about seeing Uncle Will and the news of Chris' death, but I decided to skip that too since it would've dragged out the lunch further. By then, all I wanted to do was escape.

In no frame of mind to call Vanessa, I walked down to 57th Street and blew the rest of the day shopping, but even that failed to appease my rotten mood.

Dinner with my father was scheduled the following evening at some new diner he'd found on Columbus Avenue. For all the years I remembered, he'd gone from one diner to the next ordering the same dinner, sole almandine with rice pilaf and a side of broccoli.

I said, "Dad, why don't you try something else—swiss steak or oven roasted chicken or something?"

He shrugged and for a brief moment the tension faded from his face. "I'm the proverbial old dog," he said, chuckling.

Not even two minutes later, he started, "Grace, please, as a favor to me, will you call Vanessa?"

I saw his plaintive stare and felt my throat close hard on the realization that I wouldn't do it. A dull ache bubbled behind my eyes. "You have to stop bringing this up," I said in a strained whisper. "We can't keep having this same conversation."

Then silence. We eked out a few meaningless words back and forth, but a pervasive awkwardness hung in the air for the rest of the meal. I barely managed to hug him good-bye and then I was gone, running to catch the cross-town bus at 86th Street, to the safety of Lila's green velour couch.

I rode the bus in a fog, sinking quickly into anxiety over the growing struggle with my father. I wanted to be transported instantly back to Phoenix, to the scorching sun and the golf courses and even Roger, that pasty wimp. I stayed on the bus past Lila's stop, getting off instead at York Avenue where I walked a block to the benches along the East River. I sat there in the fading daylight, watching the steady stream of joggers, bike riders and dog walkers, hoping to lose myself in this hodgepodge of random strangers.

My family was in shambles. I would leave tomorrow morning without having called Vanessa. I might agonize over her forever but I couldn't bulldoze my way past the visceral distrust that sat like a buried bullet in my core. As for my mother, she lived in some parallel universe populated by Herb and his grandchildren, still and forever fundamentally inadequate.

And my father . . . well, I was just never what it was about for him. His days began and ended with Vanessa and all my efforts to please him had not altered that single incontrovertible fact.

						* * *

I didn't cry the entire first year. Not once. After a few months, a heavy crushing weight suddenly filled my chest all the way up to my throat. Swallowing required an act of will. Breathing hurt. I went for an x-ray, for massages, for hypnosis. My doctor prescribed tranquilizers but nothing got me out from under it.

At night I dreamt of amputated limbs, my limbs. In my dreams, I would wake up to find one of my legs gone. One night it was a hand. Each time I was too shocked to cry. I would sit in my bed, staring in stunned silence at the bloody gaping hole. Twice I dreamt of Miss Zrinsky, her figure against a distant horizon, unreachable.

On bad mornings, I struggled my way out of bed and into the office. I threw myself into projects at work, re-designing employee satisfaction surveys, customer feed-back questionnaires, marketing plans, inter-office memo formats.

Ted began meeting me at work at the end of the day, pulling me away from my desk and back into our life together. We went out to dinner, to movies, plays and the basketball games I used to tease him about. Numb to my core, I had little interest in any of it.

Months passed. Nothing changed. One evening, Kathryn and I met at the bench outside Jamba Juice.

"You look terrible, Grace," she said.

Startled, I looked at her. "Uh . . . I'm just tired. I haven't been sleeping well."

"I have a name for you . . . a woman I want you to see. She's a friend. She's good."

"Good at what?" I asked.

Kathryn tossed her empty cup into a trash receptacle. "She's a psychologist. She has a private therapy practice."

I coughed, spilling my Mango Mantra on the front of my shirt. Kathryn handed me her napkins.

"You think I need a therapist?" I asked.

Kathryn hesitated. "Yes, I do," she said quietly.

I crumpled my cup and tossed it over to the trash. It hit the rim and fell to the sidewalk. Kathryn bent over to pick it up.

"Ted called you, didn't he?" My eyes searched her face.

She shrugged. "What does it matter? Here's a pen and a piece of paper. Her name is Elaine Froyer," she said. "Promise me you'll go."

*   *   *

Two days later, I sat in a chair facing Elaine Froyer. A woman I guessed to be in her late forties, she had a fashionable flair I hadn't expected. She wore a brightly colored print silk scarf tied at her neck, accentuating a white peasant blouse with puffy sleeves. Her short black hair was combed back off her face. Large dangling silver and moon stone earrings moved with every gesture.

"Tell me why you're here, Grace," she said, looking at me closely.

I swallowed over the lump in my throat. "I've been . . . pretty depressed . . . since my sister died," I said. I could barely hear my own voice.

"When did it happen?"

"Almost a year ago." I looked down at my shoes, navy pumps, frumpy next to Elaine's sleek black slingbacks.

"Had she been sick?"

I looked up, fascinated by the hypnotic movement of her earrings. I shook my head. "Not in the way you mean." I folded my hands in my lap, squeezing my fingers together until they hurt. "She killed herself."

A heavy, impenetrable silence snuffed out every sound in the room.

Finally, I heard Elaine's voice. "Why don't you tell me about it."

I put my hand to my throat and tried to swallow. "My father called me . . . early one morning. I was sitting at my desk eating an English muffin. He told me a neighbor of hers—Vanessa, her name was Vanessa . . . my sister's name—not the neighbor's name. Oh . . . I'm making this so complicated."

"It's okay, Grace. Go on."

"The neighbor smelled gas and called the police."

"Were you and Vanessa close?"

I pressed my hand to my chest, pushing against the weight. I shrugged. "We haven't . . . things haven't been good between us for a long time. But for many of the earlier years . . . well . . . I feel like Vanessa was woven through my veins and arteries."

"That's quite an image. Do you have other siblings?"

I shook my head. "I had a brother, but he was killed before Vanessa and I were born."

"So . . . you are the only one now. That's not an easy spot to be in. Tell me about your parents."

"I'm not . . . oh, just thinking about them exhausts me."

"Are they together?" she asked.

I shook my head. "Divorced. Almost 20 years. My parents were never happy together. At least not in my lifetime. They fought a lot, mostly over Vanessa. My father was devoted to Vanessa and my mother never forgave him for that. Or for my brother's death. She blamed him for all of it."

"Where did you fit into this picture?"

"I was . . . on the periphery. A slice of lemon at the side of the plate."

Elaine leaned toward me. "Tell me more specifically."

"Vanessa got most of the attention. Good or bad, it was always about Vanessa."

"So . . . you're telling me Vanessa was your father's favorite. Were you your mother's?"

I shook my head. "George—my brother who died—he was her favorite."

"How about now?" Elaine asked. "What's it like now?

"Well, I've been out here in Phoenix for almost two years. My family lives in New York. I've only seen them twice since I moved."

"Tell me about the last time."

"I went back for the funeral. Ted, my boyfriend, and I went and stayed at a hotel. I told my parents we were coming in late so we wouldn't have to see them before the funeral. Ted had never met them and . . . well . . . it's hard for me to be with them.

"The service was held in a small chapel on the cemetery grounds. They were both seated when we walked in, my father and Valerie . . . the woman he lives with. They were on the left side, my mother and Herb on the right. My father jumped up and walked over to me. The whole time I could feel the heat of my mother's eyes on me, waiting to see which of them I'd choose to sit with. It took me straight back to my childhood. I felt imposed upon . . . and angry, in a way that surprised me. I grabbed Ted's hand and pulled him to the back of the chapel. We sat alone, smack in the middle."

"How did that make you feel?"

"It was my sister's funeral. I felt like shit. I still feel like shit."

"Maybe we can do something about that," she said quietly.

Holding my breath, I blinked back tears of relief.

Epilogue

Ted and I were married a year later at the Phoenix courthouse with Kathryn and Ted's brother Bruce as witnesses. I told my parents a few days later.

We bought a three-bedroom condo in downtown Phoenix. I had the windows covered before we moved. No more black garbage bags. I wanted to get it right this time.

I went to New York to see my parents the week before Christmas when hopefully there would be a remnant of joy in the air. My mother was the same, distant and clueless. Photographs of Herb's growing grandchildren crowded the third shelf of her glass wall unit, right up there with pictures of us—George, Vanessa and me. We are cordial and perfunctory with each other. I am relieved to have found my way to a place approaching indifference.

My father is a different story. There's a heaviness in his step, in his face, even in his smile. Nothing seems effortless for him any more. He speaks slowly, almost as if he's digging for the words one at a time. His pain jabs at me; it sticks in my throat. But . . . there's nothing I can do. I can't sit next to him through this trial.

Ted and I are expecting a baby in April, two months from now. From the sonogram I had in December, we learned it will be a girl. A week later, sitting in a booth at the New World Diner, my father asked me if I'd name her after Vanessa.

Instantly my back stiffened. "I can't," I said. "Don't ask me to."

Abruptly, he looked away.

I swallowed hard, shaken momentarily by the icy edge of his silence. Pressing my back against the seat, I took a deep breath.

"Dad," I whispered.

He looked up at me and I saw the disappointment in his face.

"She deserves her own name," I said softly.

Made in the USA
Lexington, KY
05 September 2010